Five reasons you will love this book . . .

Join Alva in a daring adventure across the sea!

Prepare for murder, mystery, and vengeful Vikings.

Author Janina Ramirez creates a rich atmospheric setting filled with historical detail.

Stunning black-and-white illustrations by David Wyatt.

Will Alva discover the secret behind her father's disappearance?

KILSGARD
N
W
E
S
Dwarf's Finger
Giant's Finger
Kilsgard
Towards Northern England
KILSGARD

Meet the characters

Alva

Fenrir

Uncle Magnus

Alfred

Queen Aethelflaed

King Ragnall

Oxford University Press is a department of the University of Oxford.
It furthers the University's objective of excellence in research, scholarship,
and education by publishing worldwide. Oxford is a registered trade mark of
Oxford University Press in the UK and in certain other countries

First published 2019

British Library Cataloguing in Publication Data
Data available

ISBN: 978-0-19-2766359

1 3 5 7 9 10 8 6 4 2

Printed in Great Britain

Paper used in the production of this book is a natural,
recyclable product made from wood grown in sustainable forests.
The manufacturing process conforms to the environmental
regulations of the country of origin.

Use the kennings key at the back of this book to unlock
the hidden meanings behind the chapter titles.

JANINA RAMIREZ

WAY OF THE WAVES

A VIKING MYSTERY

ILLUSTRATED BY DAVID WYATT

The Moon's Wheel

Alva strained to make out anything in the pitch-black hut. The moon shone like a beacon outside. But here in the turf-covered hut only silvery streaks shimmered on the outlines of numerous eerie charms hanging from the low ceiling. A figure cackled and creaked in the far corner, but Alva wasn't scared. She had come here with a purpose.

Yet as Sigrunn, seer and sacrificer, rustled towards her, skull-like face gleaming through the shadows, Alva felt fear tingling up her arms. This woman had meant her harm in the past. Was she right to trust her with such a powerful secret now, alone, in the dark of night?

'I'm glad you came to me,' Sigrunn rasped.

She threw a heavy log on the embers of the near-dead fire, and gradually a red glow grew and spread through the hut. 'The Norns have whispered to me about you ever since you came screaming into the world, and I know you have a complex web of fate winding around you, girl.' She drew her skeletal face close enough for Alva to see the blue outlines of tattooed shapes on her skin. Dragons battled at the nape of her neck, while moon shapes overlapped with stars, circles, knots, and patterns over both her bony cheeks. She felt a chill of fear at being so close to someone she had spent her whole life cowering from. But she pulled herself as tall as she could manage and held the seer's gaze.

'I need a sleeping potion.'

'What does the reckless daughter of Bjorn want with a sleeping potion?' she croaked, her teeth gleaming like a row of tombstones in her gaping mouth. 'Is the tearaway trickster betraying her family by coming here? Is she set on some crime, or is she going to cast powerful spells on some helpless soul of Kilsgard?'

Alva knew the questions were designed to unsettle her. But, with as much confidence as she could muster, she replied, 'I need to put my wolf, Fenrir, to sleep for a day. He will be travelling with me, and will make too much noise if he is awake. I know you can make me a sleeping thorn—and I can pay you.' Reaching inside the leather bag tied to her belt, she drew out a fat red ruby. Reluctantly she handed over the glittering stone. It was the last of the treasure her father had left before he'd disappeared, and the last of her family's riches.

Sigrunn's grey eyes glinted red as she took the jewel. 'This is a fine stone,' she said. 'I should tell the Jarl and your difficult uncle of your visit here today, girl. But for such a prize I will give you what you want. And I feel I need to help you on your way, as I see many challenges in your path.' Turning towards the table she began to shift bowls, cooking pots, and herbs around noisily. 'You will need two gifts from me if you are to get your creature to sleep through a journey. The first is a spell, carved on oak, while the second is a potion you must get him to drink.'

Pulling a sliver of wood towards her, Sigrunn drew a knife from her pocket, the blade flashing in the dim light. Murmuring incantations under her breath, Alva saw her carve four unknown runes into the grain of the oak. They weren't like any other symbols she had seen before:

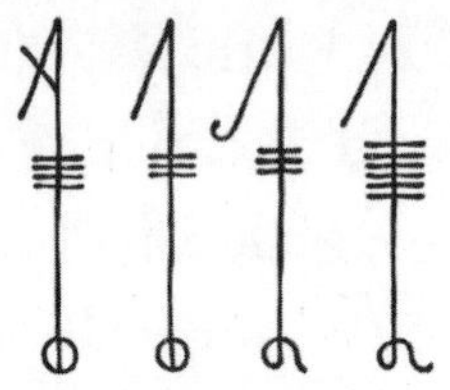

Handing her the piece of carved oak, Sigrunn said, This is the *svefnthorn.* Place this sleep tooth by the head of your wolf, and the spell will keep him in a deep slumber. But this alone will not be enough.' Drawing a small cauldron near, she busily reached for ingredients. As she poured herbs and powders, mixing them with a large wooden spoon, she spoke to Alva. 'Here is the bile of a boar and the dry leaves of the lettuce.' She added the greens to a stinking, thick, black syrup. 'Wild neep and the bite of vinegar.' A pickling sting hit the back of Alva's throat, as she choked at the pungent smell. 'And now for the poisons,' Sigrunn hissed enthusiastically.

'Poisons?' Alva asked hurriedly. 'I don't want you to poison Fen!'

'Silly girl,' the seer replied. 'I will not use enough to kill the creature. But a little hemlock, poppy seed, and mandrake are needed to make him unconscious.' She lifted three small linen

bags from a high shelf, unwrapping them and spooning out tiny amounts from each. Adding them to the pot, she then carried her concoction to the fire, placing it above the flames.

'The brew must boil. Then you will have your *dwale*—your sleeping potion.' Alva crouched next to the hearth, watching the brown liquid swirl about. 'Are you going to tell me why you need to travel with a sleeping wolf, child?' Sigrunn said. 'I'm sure your mother would not want you leaving town when Spring is coming and your help will be needed.' She gave a leering sideways smile, her knowing, age-old eyes sparkling in the firelight.

'You have my payment,' Alva answered, bristling with guilt at the old crone's words. 'I will tell you no more. Where I go and what I do is my business alone.'

Sigrunn replied with a slow, low cackle.

Reduced now to silence, they could hear the liquid inside the cauldron begin to bubble. 'It is ready,' Sigrunn said, rising from her stool. She carried the potion over to the table, pulling forward a small glass container. Placing a funnel in the spout, she slowly poured the steaming, smelly concoction into the bottle, before pushing a stopper firmly in the mouth. 'Your beast will not want to drink this as it tastes foul. You must mix up some fine meat and pour the potion on top. Once he has eaten he will begin to feel sleepy, and then you have from morning till night before he awakes.'

'Are you absolutely sure the poisons won't harm him?' Alva asked nervously.

Cackling again, Sigrunn replied, 'I've given double this dose to Viking heroes and they have risen healthy and well after the night.'

She threw the leftover mixture on to the fire, and a pungent smoke engulfed the hut. 'Now leave me, child of Bjorn. I will not speak of this for now, but if you ever vex me again I will inform the town of your night-journey here.'

Gathering up her belongings, Alva wrapped the small vial safely and slipped it inside her pouch. Exiting the hut, she whispered back at the hunched figure in the doorway. 'Thanks to you, Seer Sigrunn, and thanks to the All-Father.'

Fenrir was waiting outside, and gave a nervous whimper as he saw Alva emerge.

'It's okay, Fen,' she said, ruffling the soft, silver fur on the top of his head. 'I have your medicine, and now we can begin our adventure!'

She spoke with more enthusiasm than she felt. This was going to be dangerous. Really dangerous. She could end up humiliated, exiled, or worse. But she had to follow the feeling that filled her like a horn cup ready to overflow. She had to take to the waves. She had to find her father.

Horse of the Mountains of the Swans

With Fenrir as her shadow, Alva made her way back towards Kilsgard, occasionally running her fingers over the smooth glass container in her pouch. She had done it! She'd managed to get Sigrunn to help her. Her heart was racing with excitement and pride. But she knew that the real work started now.

As the fortified walls of the town appeared, Alva turned a sharp left, away from the safety of her home. Instead she moved towards the sea. All was calm now, but she knew at first light the waters would be churned into a frenzy as five ships hurried to leave the harbour; full of men ready to go a-Viking.

And she would be on one of those ships.

She had planned this for weeks now, ever since she heard her Uncle Magnus and Jarl Erik discussing a trip to England. They were to return two Anglo-Saxons and a precious relic to the island of Lindisfarne, in return for a huge ransom. Then the men would perhaps raid and trade a little in England before returning home. But Alva would not return with them. She was on a longer mission: to find her missing father. He had disappeared from his raiding party over a year ago, but she was convinced that he was still alive and that she would find him.

It had been hard saying goodbye. Her family had no idea of her plans, and that evening Alva had struggled to hide her true feelings. Holding her mother's hand a little too long, she had felt tears prick behind her eyes. Brianna would be alone now, bringing up Alva's little brother Ivan with no help.

She felt consumed with guilt thinking back to her last hours at home with her family. Grabbing a hunk of Fenrir's fur in her fist, she remembered that right now she wasn't alone. She had her best friend, her sniffer-wolf assistant, and her protector here with her.

The soil beneath their feet changed to sand,

which crunched under the soles of Alva's shoes. They were at the shore. A magical sight met her. Five dragon-prowed longships were outlined against the black water. Their eyes were picked out in gold, and as they bobbed up and down on the waves it seemed to Alva as if they were winking at her. By their side stood a cloaked figure, white hair reaching far down his back. As he turned, the moonlight illuminated his face. It was full of creases and crags, like a mountain range, and a beard hung down to his waist like a scarf from his skinny jaw. Small yet muscular, skinny yet sturdy, old yet with a youthful twinkle in his eye, he welcomed Alva.

'Child,' he said in a gravelly voice, 'I'm so glad you are here in time. I have already seen the shimmer of morning edging along the sky.'

'Hello, Olaf,' Alva said quietly. She had spent many days with this strange old man: shipbuilder, poet, and font of much knowledge. 'I got a potion and a spell to keep Fen quiet on the journey.' She felt excitement ringing through her skin despite the heavy feelings of guilt and regret that still swirled around her stomach. 'I can't believe this is really happening!'

'You must stay quiet,' he hissed. 'I know you

are excited, but we have much to do and much to prepare. I've one last thing for you before you leave for the sea.' He took a bag from his waist and drew out an object wrapped in leather. As he unfurled it Alva gasped. He held towards her a cube of crystal about the size of her palm. Its sides were perfectly smooth, and, most incredible of all, the stone was clear like water.

'This is a sunstone, Alva,' Olaf murmured through his heavy beard. 'I gave one to your father, and now I give one to you. You two are so alike—both like caged wolves desperate to run and explore. This stone is incredibly rare and valuable; it was given to me in exchange for a ship. I hope that with its help you will find your father and return to Kilsgard.'

Hugging Olaf tightly around the waist, Alva thought about how much this stone was worth. A ship in payment! The time, effort, and sheer amount of stuff needed to build a longship were extraordinary, so she must treasure this gift. It was worth a small fortune, and she ached with gratitude towards the kind shipbuilder. 'What's it for?' she asked him.

'You will be very valuable to the men on your ship with this stone, Alva,' Olaf replied. 'With this you can navigate even if the sun has vanished and the stars are not there to guide you. When clouds cover the sky, hold this to your eye and you will see the outline of the sun. This means you can keep your ship on course and not be lost at sea. This stone will keep you safe. Well, the stone and that huge silver creature you insist on taking with you.'

They both looked at Fenrir. 'It's nearly time, I think,' said Alva. 'We've got to get him loaded into the barrel before the first men arrive.' She looked sadly at the wolf by her feet. She didn't want to give him Sigrunn's potion, but under no circumstances was she leaving him behind. No, she and Fenrir were one and the same. Where she went, he went.

'You are crazy to bring that beast on a ship,' Olaf said. 'The men will think Ragnarök itself has begun when it leaps out in the middle of the sea.' But he gave a slight smile as he scolded her.

'Is everything prepared?' she asked.

'I left that water barrel empty and put some blankets inside to keep you warm. I've placed some dried sardines and bread in there, along with a skin of water, so you won't perish. There is plenty of meat on board the ship, but you'll not get to enjoy it, as you'll probably be thrown overboard the second they discover you've stowed away.'

'I can persuade them to keep me on the voyage,' Alva replied. With a cheeky glint in her eye, she said, 'They know I am cunning, quick, and clever. Plus, I have this stone now and a great big wolf to defend me.' Alva gave Olaf a mischievous grin, which made her cheeks round like apples, speckled with freckles. He pulled her into his chest, hugging her tight.

Full of excitement, she and Olaf chopped up chunks of steak, covered them with Sigrunn's potion, and encouraged Fenrir to eat every bit. The draught worked surprisingly quickly. As the poor wolf's legs buckled underneath him, Alva felt a pang of worry for her beloved friend and prayed to the gods that he would wake again. Olaf lifted the now-sleeping beast into the barrel, and they placed the sleep tooth spell under his head before Alva climbed in after him. Thankfully, the barrel was large, designed to hold water for the crew on the seas. They would be livid when they realized this one was empty, so Olaf had hidden a second full water barrel on board. Food they could do without, but water they could not.

Before lifting the heavy lid into place, sealing her in darkness, Olaf whispered, 'It's not too late to change your mind. It will be hard at sea and you may never return to Kilsgard. Are you sure you are ready?'

Alva looked into Olaf's misty eyes. 'If I stay here I will never be what I am meant to be. I need to see the world before I am tied to a hearth like my mother. I am a shield maiden. I have a ship here, and the world my uncle has told me of—wise men where the sun burns bright, books with the secrets of eternal life inside, and princesses who rule like men—is just a journey away.'

Olaf wiped a tear from the corner of one creased eye. 'You will be so missed, so very missed, by many here. But I know what compels you. You are your father's daughter!' He gave her hand a final squeeze, then she was plunged into darkness. Alva could just hear his voice through the thick wood. 'This will be your home as you travel the seas. Respect the ship and it will respect you. May the gods keep you safe.'

The Fish Field

She was trying not to panic. But it felt like the wooden walls were slowly closing in, crushing her. With each rock of the waves—up, down, up, down—her stomach lurched. She wanted to be sick but knew she would then have to sit trapped inside the barrel alongside her own vomit.

Her mind was swimming with regrets now the first thrill of being at sea had passed. At first it was so exciting, hearing the men arriving, traipsing on to the ships and checking the supplies. Her heart had been in her mouth as someone stood next to her barrel and shouted to Olaf, 'Is this the water? Is it full?' He had replied confidently that there would be plenty of water to get to Lindisfarne and back if necessary, but

Alva had waited tensely in case the man prised up the lid to check inside.

She heard sails unfurling, ropes heaving, oars splashing as the ship's captain, Grim, counted off the men's strokes. 'Heave! Heave! Heave!' he bellowed. Inside the barrel, Alva pressed herself close to Fenrir as her insides swirled with each movement. After some time, she heard Grim again, 'Now rest your oars,' and the splashing stopped. The chatter of twenty men drifted over to her as the sails took the strain, carrying the ship further out to sea. Among the voices one cut through clear and loud: her Uncle Magnus.

Alva had arranged with Olaf that she would be on the same ship as her uncle. While she knew it would mean a storm of fury crashing down when she revealed herself on board, she hoped that he would eventually soften and look after her. She understood Magnus's moods well. He often scolded Alva, pointing out when her hair was a mess, or when she had behaved particularly recklessly. But he did love her.

These thoughts didn't make the pain of leaving her home any easier, though. Her last memories of her warm, safe hut in Kilsgard were of her mother looking beautiful and happy in the light of the fire, and Ivan running over and giving her an unexpected hug before going down to sleep. She loved her family, but now she was far at sea, with just echoes of their faces in her mind.

Alva had been listening intently to the talk of the men on board and estimated that they had been tossing about on the waves for what must be half a day now. Alva felt Fenrir's chest to make sure he was still sleeping. The wolf hadn't moved for the whole journey, and Alva sent thoughts of thanks to Sigrunn for her spell and potion. Yet she sensed he would wake up soon. She had to reveal herself to the men on board before they were startled by the waking howls of Fen.

It was quiet on board right now. Their skins of water would soon be empty, they would turn their minds to the barrel, and she would be discovered. They must be a long distance from Kilsgard, and there was no chance they would take her back. She had to show herself. Olaf had made the lid of the barrel loose enough for her to push open from the inside. Swallowing hard, steeling herself, Alva gave it a shove.

Thump! The sound of the wood hitting the deck was impossible to ignore. 'What's that?'

shouted a gruff voice nearby. An even nearer voice replied, 'It's just the lid of the water barrel. I'll fix it back on.' Alva heard six huge footsteps, then looked up to see an enormous bearded face staring down at her. There was a long pause, as the cheerful eyes of Grim himself went dead, before a look of startled recognition crept across his face.

'By Thor!' the captain exclaimed. 'Is that . . . Alva?' She froze as if she was cowering at the feet of the thunder-god himself. Another pause, then Grim raised his voice high above the waves, 'Magnus! By all the gods . . . Magnus! Come here! Look!'

Scuffling and more footsteps beside the barrel. Then Alva's insides curled around themselves as Magnus's shocked face appeared framed against the dull white sky above her. Like Grim, he seemed confused at first. But then the fire-god Surtr could not have burned with rage any more. Furious, he reached in, grabbing Alva by the shoulders and dragging her on to the ship's deck.

She caught her elbow on the oak planks as she landed, and felt a small stream of warm blood trickle down her arm. 'Alva!' Magnus yelled. 'In

all the nine realms, there can be no explanation as to why you are on board this ship!'

'Owww!' Alva yelled. 'You've hurt me!'

'Hurt you?!' Magnus said menacingly. 'Girl, you're lucky I haven't killed you already! How did you . . .? What about your mother? Oh, Alva, you reckless, thoughtless child! What can we do with you now?' He was pacing up and down in front of her as he spoke, thoughts and words tumbling over each other.

The rest of the crew had been shocked into silence, but now Grim checked himself and stepped forward. 'Magnus, we are on an important mission for Jarl Erik. We must get to Lindisfarne and return with the ransom payment. There is no way we can have a young girl with us. We will have to take her back.'

There were groans from the other men. No one wanted to make the return journey as they had been at sea for nearly a day now. 'We can't turn back, Grim,' Magnus replied. 'The waves are building and we will be fighting against them if we attempt to head to Kilsgard.' Raising his fist to the angry clouds above he shouted, 'What mischief will you deliver us next, Loki?!'

Turning back to Alva, he drew her close to

him, grabbing the fur on the cloak around her neck. His grey eyes were flashing with sparks, like hammers on an anvil. 'I know why you are here, Alva. You think you can travel with me to discover what happened to Bjorn all those moons ago. But you are selfish. You seek this adventure, yet you've left your poor mother and brother alone to struggle through the season. I am very disappointed in you.'

He let her go, and Alva slumped back against the barrel, feeling shot through the heart. She knew the words from her uncle would hurt, but he was not holding back. He was furious with her.

'Uncle,' she said cautiously. 'I planned this carefully. I can be of assistance to you and the men. I have been learning about ships from Olaf, and he gave me something you may find useful on this voyage.'

'Pah!' Magnus spat. 'Bjorn told us all of mad Olaf and his weird ways. Anyone would think ships are gods the way he talks about them. What could he possibly have given you that can help a ship full of seasoned seafarers?'

Smirking slightly, but covering her face with her wild head of flaming red hair so her uncle couldn't see, Alva drew the wrapped gift from her pouch. The men watched in silence.

Unwrapping the stone, Alva watched as their eyes twinkled with childlike excitement. One huge, lumbering man whispered with a childish giggle, 'A sunstone! The girl has a sunstone!'

Another replied hurriedly, 'This is very strange! Bjorn has saved us on many a voyage with his stone, but how can his child have one too?'

Grim stepped forward, grabbing the stone from Alva's hands. 'With this we can keep our course even if this storm that's brewing crashes around us. She has brought us a valuable navigation tool. This is a gift from Odin, who wants us to see in the dark. She must stay aboard. She must travel with us to England.'

The Heart of the Earth

Grim turned the stone over and over in his fat fingers, then held it up to the sky. 'See!' he exclaimed with excitement. 'The sun burns through the clouds here. We won't be lost at sea again!'

Turning to Alva he said, 'We are too far to turn back now anyway, and with this stone you have suddenly become very useful, young Alva. But how did you get such a treasure? These jewels are rare and can only be found in the mountains of the icy North.'

Alva replied quietly, 'Olaf was given two by a traveller. He gave one to my father, and one to me.' Then more quietly still, 'Perhaps it pays to listen to the ramblings of a madman now and again.'

The snipe wasn't lost on Magnus, whose bat-like senses meant that he could hear Alva's mistakes almost before she made them. 'Think you can afford to be cheeky, do you, Alva? We'll see how cheeky you feel when you get a look over the side of the ship. The men are within their rights to throw you overboard!'

Still furious, he grabbed her again. Alva struggled as Magnus dragged her away from the barrel, to where the angry black waves were leaping high against the sides. Panic rose within her. Surely her uncle wouldn't throw her overboard? She grunted, wriggled, and howled, as the other men gave contrasting shouts of, 'You do it, Magnus!' and, 'No, let her go!'

But their shouts suddenly turned to shrieks as from out of the barrel a huge, fanged silver beast leapt up, pouncing on Magnus and pinning him to the wooden deck. Fenrir was snarling, showing glinting sharp teeth, and a strand of dribble dropped on Magnus's face as the wolf breathed hot and loud above him, his paws pinning down each shoulder.

Amongst the chaos, Magnus had released Alva. She calmly stood up, dusted down her tunic, and spoke. 'Fen, it's okay. It's just

Magnus.' At her words, Fenrir's eyes switched from wild woodland beast to playful puppy. He wagged his tail and drew a long, wet tongue over Magnus's face. Then he playfully bounded back towards Alva, his feet still a little wobbly from the sleeping potion. She threw her arms around his wide neck and whispered in his ear, 'Thanks for saving me.'

Fen snuggled into her for a moment, then froze. Alva looked at him closely. He had turned solid as his eyes took in the ship, the waves, the confused bearded men. Realization was dawning. He was at sea. Leaping away from Alva, he spun in the air, howling uncontrollably. First he dashed for the end of the boat, as strong arms grabbed at him, then, clambering up to the dragon-headed prow, he cowered, shot terrified gazes around at the ocean, and hared blindly back towards Alva. Buckets, ropes, oars all went flying in his wake.

'Fen!' Alva cried. 'Calm down! Come to me!' But the wolf was caught in a game of cat and mouse as each of the men on board took turns to corner him. At last, Sigurd, one of the younger men, who was tall with long, wavy blond hair and seemed to be made entirely of muscle, got the wolf pinned against the side. But Fenrir made one last bid for freedom, turning on the spot and leaping into the water.

As he fell towards the wild sea, his paws caught in a loose rope hanging off the deck and wrapped around his silver fur. Huge eyes full of fear, howling, he plunged into the freezing waves. He began struggling for air, as his head bobbed above and below the waterline.

'Fen!' Alva screamed. 'I'll help you. Just stop wriggling.' But it was no good. The wolf was thrashing from side to side, and each movement wound the thick rope more firmly round his limbs.

Alva looked around in desperation. She pulled off her cloak, tossed her shoes to one side, and stood up, ready to jump into the water. She leant forward, reached out her arms, and cried out, 'Fen, I'm coming!'

Then she felt a biting grip on her wrist. Alva turned to see Magnus, bare chested, pushing past her. Magnus made for the side and vaulted over the edge. Alva stood amazed as her uncle of forty winters moved towards Fen with the speed and agility of one of the elf-folk.

'What are you doing?' Alva screeched at him,

but the sound was lost in the tumultuous waves that threatened to whip her uncle and wolf away to sea. She could barely watch. Magnus nearly grasped the silvery fur, but another wave dragged the exhausted wolf beneath the water. Alva let out a scream as Fenrir sank and disappeared under the green-blue surface. 'He's gone! He's drowning!' she cried with anguish.

Letting go of the side of the boat, Magnus hit the water with a great splash. In an instant, he too had plunged below the waves. Alva couldn't move. She couldn't breathe. She just stood rooted to the spot repeating silent prayers to Freya, Thor, Odin . . . 'Gods and goddesses, let my wolf survive.' She could hear each heartbeat as a death drum.

Then, finally, Magnus sprang above the surface of the water, his beard whipping around like a fish on a hook. In his arms was Fenrir, limp and unmoving. He tied the immobile creature to the bottom of the rope, clambered over him up to the deck of the ship, then began to haul the wolf from the water.

'Is he breathing? Is he alive?' Alva called out. Then she heard a faint whimper. Magnus stood up, and by his side was a wet, worried, and weary-looking Fenrir—soaked and slippery, but definitely alive.

Alva again flung her arms around Fenrir and buried her face in his wet, smelly fur. 'Thank you,' she said to her uncle. 'You saved him.'

Slumping down next to her, Magnus put a strong, wet arm around her shoulder. Sighing, he said, 'Alva, you will be the death of me.'

The men, relieved at the rescue, brought blankets and cups of mead to them, while Sigurd rubbed Fen's shivering fur dry. It was strange seeing handsome, strong Sigurd petting her wolf. Both their fathers had left to go a-Viking last year. Sigurd's father, Ulf, had been one of her father's best friends. Now neither of them knew where their fathers were. Alva felt relief slowly wash through her, as together with Sigurd, she felt Fenrir's heartbeat slow down.

'I'm sorry, Uncle,' Alva said to Magnus.

'I know you are, Alva. You are always sorry when you do something wrong. One day you'll learn to do as you're told, to do what's expected of you. But that day is not today. Today, it seems, you are going a-Viking.'

Wide Awning of the Cloud Halls

A reluctant calm settled on board the ship over the next day or so. Magnus was still silently fuming at Alva, but the drama of Fen's rescue had brought a truce between them. Grim paced up and down the prow of the boat, murmuring from time to time that the mission would be compromised by having a young girl on board, but Sigurd and some of the other men did all they could to make her comfortable.

Many of the older men on board were fathers in Kilsgard and had known Alva since she was a babe. She had played with their children and grown up under their watchful eyes. They wanted her to feel as safe as possible in the middle of the wild sea. Alva felt a rush of gratitude every time one of them brought her a cup of water, ruffled Fen's fur, or wrapped a blanket tighter round her shoulders. These were good men, and she was safe with them.

But the sea was turning yet more wild. Alva made herself as useful as she could on board, cleaning, preparing food, distributing water, and tending to the ropes. She tried her hand at an oar, but the weight was too great and she simply couldn't keep pace with the trained strokes of the others. They had left Kilsgard with blue skies, but the further towards England they travelled, the darker the clouds became.

Two days into the journey they felt the first rain. The ship was already cramped, uncomfortable, smelly, but the added discomfort of being soaked to the skin affected Alva's mood. She hid beneath canopies when she could, consoling Fenrir, who despised every second his paws were on this moving wooden sea beast. He'd been terribly seasick, vomiting regularly on the decks. Alva was charged with cleaning this up and keeping the wolf away from the men, but the rain had made Fen even more unhappy.

The waves grew darker, taller, and began to

smash inside the ship. With each surge the decks became a lake. Along with four others, Alva spent hours, bucket in hand, scooping up water and tossing it back into the sea. Her arms ached from her labours, her back ached from sleeping on rough wooden boards, and her heart ached with longing for the comforts of her home. Yet it was getting darker still.

The ship had left Kilsgard with four other longships, each staying in sight of one another and following the course set for Lindisfarne. They had at times come close enough for the seafarers to shout instructions and updates across at one another, while at other times they were simply dots on the horizon. But despite the weather and the waves, the five ships remained bound for England together.

Yet, on the third evening at sea, as the rain began to lash harder on the ship, and the clouds turned solid black, it became harder to make out the other boats. The waves doubled in height and threw Alva up and down. Only Olaf's remarkable craftsmanship and the wide berth of the ship kept it from capsizing. As the wind became a howling gale, the men drew in the sail and began to row feverishly to keep moving towards the coast of

England. But they soon realized this was futile and exhaustedly joined Alva and Fen beneath the tar-lined canopies, crying oaths to the gods and huddling together for warmth.

Alva had never felt so terrified. She had experienced more drama, fear, and excitement than many girls her age. But the thought that any second the wide jaws of the sea would snap her up for eternity filled her with a hollow, empty dread. She couldn't stop shaking. Every limb ached from the repeated shivering that she had no control over. Fenrir's fear fed her own, as his usually comforting warm body lay cold and distant next to hers. The face of her mother and brother crept regularly into her disorientated mind, and at times she imagined she could smell hot lamb broth on the hearth, or hear her mother's gentle singing while Alva buried her face in soft woollen sheets on the bed in her home. This was the worst decision she had ever made. She hated being on the sea and would trade an arm to be back in the comfort of Kilsgard.

It felt like the storm lasted an eternity. The men tried to keep spirits up by singing rousing tavern songs, spinning sagas, and boasting about times at sea that had been far worse than this. They sowed seeds of hope, announcing that the wind was calming, or the clouds were parting, only for another fierce stormy assault to silence their words. Alva knew they were all afraid. Only Magnus remained silent and strong.

He said little to Alva, keeping his words and thoughts to himself. At times he would draw an unfamiliar object from his bag, which Alva knew had all manner of fascinating objects from his many travels concealed inside. He would examine a crystal, stare at a piece of parchment, fiddle with a mechanical device. He said barely anything to her. She yearned for a comforting word, a touch, an encouraging phrase. But Alva knew that Magnus was full of anger and regret that she was on board the ship in the first place. If they went down in the storm then Brianna would lose husband, brother-in-law, and daughter in the space of one year. It was too much for Alva to bear.

With no energy left she drifted into a troubled sleep, resigned to whatever fate the Norns had in store. Her dreams were a spiralling cauldron of images, some happy memories but mixing and blending with bizarre spectral faces that screamed at her. They were Mother, Maiden, Krone—the three *wyrd* sisters of fate shouting at her repeatedly through her sleep. The dizzying nightmare finally broke when she felt a firm hand slap her on the cheek.

'Alva, wake up!' Magnus was looking down at her. 'You're in a fever. You must drink this.' He pushed a horn of stinking liquid towards her, and she gagged at the smell.

'It's disgusting,' she wretched, pushing the cup away.

'Ha! There's my stubborn shield maiden,' Magnus said, his eyes glinting slightly. 'You must drink it. The storm is passing, and now we need your fever to pass too.'

Reluctantly, Alva dragged herself into a sitting position. Her head was pounding with all the drums of Asgard, and she felt disorientated. Magnus helped her up, his now kind, strong arms bringing a warm sense of calm that spread through her like a tonic. She downed the foul liquid in one, swallowing hard to keep it inside. Leaning back on her uncle's chest, she felt his breathing through his furs. It was regular, relaxed, soothing. She fell back into sleep, but this time no terrifying faces screeched at her in the darkness.

Fair Jewel of the High Storm-House

The next time Alva opened her eyes, the scene around her was very different. The men were all up and busying themselves, tying ropes, folding away canopies, and raising the sail with loud whooshing sounds. 'The rain has stopped,' Grim said as he hurried past her. 'We have got to make up lost time, but we can't see the other ships. I'm not even sure they survived the storm.' Looking up, Alva could see that the sky was still dark, despite being drier and calmer.

'Can we catch up with them?' she asked the exhausted captain.

'If they made it through the storm ahead of us, they may already have reached land. We've been blown off course, as we had to stop rowing and travel with the waves,' he replied. Bending down on one knee in front of Alva, he lowered his voice. 'Alva, this is the moment for you to show the men they were right to keep you on board this ship. We need your sunstone. We must find out what direction we are travelling and set our sails for the coast of England. But the sun is still behind clouds, and we cannot wait to follow the stars tonight.'

Alva immediately reached into her pouch and, without thinking, handed the precious cube to Grim. These men had protected her, reassured her, and kept her alive. They had every right to use her sunstone. Grim gave her a grateful smile then raced over to the prow, drawing the jewel from its wrapping and placing it to his eye. Everyone stopped what they were doing and stared at him. 'It's the sunstone,' Sigurd called, his blue eyes turning wide with anticipation. 'Can you see the sun, Grim?'

After a long pause, Grim lowered the stone, a slow smile crawling over his face. 'It's there!' He pointed towards a particularly dense patch of clouds. The others strained but could see nothing.

'Are you sure?' Sigurd replied. 'I can't see it.'

'I'm certain! It appeared like a vision through the crystal. We are travelling in the wrong direction entirely. As it is after noon, the sun is in the west. We are travelling south. Set a new course. All men to the oars!' he cried loudly. 'We must steer westward again. Alva, I will need to hold on to the stone, as we must keep the sun in view at all times. We cannot afford to drift any further south or we will find ourselves in the hostile territories of our enemies.'

The men began to turn the prow gradually more northwards, as Grim instructed the men on the left of the boat to give hard strokes. With the dragon head pointing towards Grim's invisible sun, they set into a steady pace, and Alva felt the energy on board tingling with anticipation.

Magnus spoke suddenly in her ear. 'This is dangerous, Alva. We were expected in Lindisfarne, but now we have no idea where we may land. Let us just hope it is somewhere the people are sympathetic to Norse seafarers; otherwise we could find ourselves in considerable trouble.'

This was the fourth day at sea, so the edges of England should be drawing close. Their supplies were running low, as they were only expecting to be at sea for a handful of days. And they had no idea if their mission was still possible: the Lindisfarne relics could have been lost in the storm, perhaps they were now lying on the sea bed. Deep in thought, Alva found Fenrir bravely peering over the edge of the ship towards the stern, and, standing with her hand in the deep fur on his back, she took up watch with him, waiting to see if land would appear along the horizon.

'Land!' she cried after a short while. A shimmer of green crept into vision, and Alva was sure she could see a curl of smoke. She was suddenly desperate to get off the boat, to feel solid earth beneath her feet, to release her mind from the constant swirling of the waves. But if they were nearing land, they were also approaching people—potentially hostile people. The men slowed their strokes, and Magnus joined Grim at the prow to examine the coastline.

'There is a great opening from sea into river,' Magnus said. 'I believe we may be approaching what the Anglo-Saxons call the "Hymbra", the river that snakes all the way to . . .' he dropped off, casting a knowing glance at Grim. But Sigurd finished the sentence for him. Excitedly he shouted, 'Jorvik! We're heading for Jorvik!

Oh, Alva,' he said, rushing over to her and grabbing her hands, 'you are going to see the greatest Viking city in England!'

'Calm down, Sigurd,' Magnus said impatiently. 'You know this is not good news. Firstly, we are now more than a day's sailing from Lindisfarne. Secondly, Jorvik is currently under the control of King Ragnall—he they call "the King of the Light Foreigners and the Dark Foreigners".' Sigurd and some of the other men gave a low hiss. 'We may not get a warm welcome from him, as he has long been an outcast in search of a kingdom. At least we will meet with other Norsemen in Jorvik, however. And we need supplies and news, so we must put our trust in Fate.'

Grim ordered the men to pick up speed with their oars, and they began a gradual approach to land. Leaving the sea behind, their stealthy ship wound carefully along a fast-flowing wide river. Magnus joined Alva, a look of excitement in his eyes. 'It is many years since I travelled along this river. It has a funny ancient name. The English call it "Use", which in their old tongue meant "wet river"!' Looking into the waters he gave a chuckle. 'You have to agree with them. The river is certainly wet.' Alva felt a great rush of happiness at hearing her uncle joking with her. Their journey had taken a strange turn, but the promise of even greater adventure made her skin hum with excitement. She threw a wide grin at Magnus. It was the happiest she had felt since leaving Kilsgard.

The men travelled carefully and quietly along the river. They told her that the south bank was full of men who hated Norse travellers, while the north bank was ruled by the fierce and notorious King Ragnall. They spun tales of Ragnall's exploits. How he had been exiled from the great Viking city of Dublin. He had wandered and warred his way across the Western Isles and Scotland, before reclaiming the great Viking city of Jorvik and declaring himself king. He was ruthless, brutal, and, some said, cruel. Alva was used to kind rulers like Jarl Erik. She was a little wary at the thought of this war-loving warrior.

The river wound the ship further inland, and, as the sun was turning the sky a dusky pink, the atmosphere among the men grew heightened. The green fields gave way to wooden and thatched buildings pressed up close to where the bank met the water. The sounds changed from the occasional bleat of sheep to a cacophony of noise. From deep within the dense wooden buildings Alva could hear playful shrieks of children, hammering of tools, and a mixture of human and animal noises all layered on top of one another. This place must be five times the size of Kilsgard.

The harbour drew into view, with twenty or more ships pressed up against one another. Huts were dispersed along the waterside, and people and goods were squeezed along gangplanks. Faces turned towards them as their dragon prow crept closer to the bay. An extremely fat man with a short spiky beard, a red tunic, and a large golden brooch on his chest began waving at them. 'The harbour master,' Grim murmured. 'Where does he want us to dock? There's surely no room?'

'He's guiding us between those two ships,' Magnus offered up. 'It'll be a squeeze.'

Grim ordered the men to draw their oars in while he completed the complicated job of steering into the narrow space. The ships either side of Alva reached up to twice the height of their modest boat. They were designed to carry

far more men and goods, and they boasted lavish decoration carved on their sides that made Olaf's humble vessel look like a rustic rowing boat. This was clearly a city teeming with wealth and riches.

The prow bumped solidly against the gangplank, and immediately the fat man with the golden brooch appeared in front of them. 'Where have you travelled from and where are you bound for?' he asked in a heavily accented Norse that Alva had to strain to understand.

Grim replied proudly, 'We are men of Jarl Erik of Kilsgard in the northern fjords. We are on a mission for our Jarl to the small island of Lindisfarne, a day's sail north of here. But a storm hit us and we sailed for the safety of Ragnall's court in Jorvik. We just require time to replenish our supplies, discover news of the other ships we travelled with, and find a safe place to rest a while.'

The man on the wharf answered back. 'You are fortunate to find yourselves in Jorvik. There is much warfare throughout these kingdoms at the moment, and it is not a safe place for men of the North. My name is Thorskill. You must travel with me straight to the King's hall. He will want oaths from you tonight.'

The men began to gather belongings, and, as a skinny boy beside the harbour master tossed up a plank of wood, Grim led them across it to dry land. Alva pulled her furs up tighter around her ears and drew Fenrir close to her side. Magnus walked behind her, whispering, 'We cannot be sure a young girl and a wolf will be given a warm welcome. Stay near me.'

It was a strange sensation as Alva's feet stood firmly on the shore. She had become so used to the pulse and surge of the waves that she immediately felt like the ground was swimming beneath her. Dizzy and sick, she grabbed on to Magnus's arm for support. He gave her a knowing smile. 'You'll be all right in a moment. Just try to keep to a straight line and soon your body will adjust.'

She kept her head down as they walked past Thorskill, but he thrust out a wide arm, stopping her and Magnus in their tracks. 'What is this?' he said, pointing at Fenrir. Grim appeared beside them, full of explanations. 'This young girl is my most trusted companion's niece. She has been useful to us, and her beast is no threat. He is fully under her command.'

Thorskill looked thoughtfully at Fenrir, who gazed back with wide, innocent eyes. 'I've heard of men taming wolves as pets, but never a young girl.' He turned a curious glance at Alva. 'How many winters have you seen, child?'

'Thirteen,' Alva replied cautiously.

'To have travelled on a longship you must be as wild as your beast. Will you cause trouble here in Jorvik?' Thorskill asked.

'I will be no trouble at all, I promise,' Alva replied, crossing her fingers behind her back.

Terrifying Lord of Princes

They fell into single file, following the surprisingly swift pace set by the huge harbour master. Alva had to take nearly three trots to every one of the men's strides, and Fenrir stayed close to her heels. Slightly out of breath, she gasped at what she saw around her. Jorvik was the most exciting, unusual, and fascinating place she had ever seen. It was as if Kilsgard had become giant-sized.

Most of the buildings were not unfamiliar, made in a similar way to those in her home town, of wood and plaster. But instead of turf on the roofs, here there was thatch. And they were much thinner and longer. The sheer number of houses overwhelmed her, as there was virtually no space to even squeeze between them.

The stink of the leatherworkers' yard blended with the rancid smell of the butchers and fishmongers. The clang of metal rang out from the blacksmiths, while Alva's ears tried to untangle the many accents and languages she heard spoken around her. Norse mixed with Old English, but more exotic tongues wound their way through the noise too.

As they raced along the busy road from the wharf, an impressive stone building reared up behind the wooden houses. Alva had heard about churches but had never seen one. The one appearing in front of her now seemed enormous! She stopped in her tracks. Magnus noticed, grabbing her by the hand and pulling her along to keep step with the others. 'That building is . . .' She trailed off as she spoke, overwhelmed by the huge stone tower she could just see above the rooftops.

'That building is known as the Minster,' Magnus said, a note of awe in his voice. 'There have been Christians living and working in that place for many hundreds of years. The church is known throughout the world for its clever monks and its collection of books. But we can't explore it right now. We must head for the King's hall. I'll take you to the Minster soon if I can.'

He shuffled her along, and the huddle of houses suddenly opened to an unexpectedly wide space, at the heart of which stood an impressive oak palace. Doors three times Alva's height stood open in front of her. Official-looking men and women scurried through the doorway, all busily humming around the heart of the city: the King's hall.

Jarl Erik's hall looked like a shed in comparison. Huge gables reached high above the surrounding rooftops, and bright paints picked out carved scenes on the entrance. Over the door, Alva could see the story of Sigurd, the hero who defeated the dragon Fafnir, drank his blood, and then could understand the language of the birds. Here the heroic Sigurd wrestled with the dragon, their bodies picked out in reds, greens, and blues, while the beast's eyes and hero's sword—named Gram—glittered in gold. As the group came to a halt outside the hall, two of the men nudged their own Sigurd and pointed upwards. 'Your namesake is here,' one mumbled. 'Wonder if you'll have to battle a dragon today too.' Shuffling and laughter came from the group, quickly silenced by the harbour master, Thorskill, who raised his voice above the noise.

'I will announce your arrival in the hall. All weapons must be left outside as is usual when in the company of a ruler, and you must not speak to the King unless he speaks to you first. You must call him "My lord" and you must pay him all due respect.' His speech over, Thorskill walked through the doors, and the men of Kilsgard looked at each other nervously.

Grim spoke to them. 'Listen to the man,' he said. 'We are here in Jorvik without invitation. We need the King's hospitality if we are to continue our mission, and he is known to be an impatient ruler. Hold your tongues and bear yourselves well.'

Thorskill appeared back at the entrance and gestured Grim forward. 'You may enter now. The King is not pleased to have a shipload of Norsemen in his city, but he knows of Jarl Erik and the men of Kilsgard. He will see you for a moment.'

Grim sorted the men into line, removing their swords and knives and straightening their clothes. He put Alva and Magnus at the back but looked at Fenrir. 'This creature can't come into the hall. Alva, you will have to leave him here. He can guard our weapons.'

Fen looked up with round, concerned eyes at Alva. She knew Grim was right. The King would not want a wolf in his hall, no matter how tame he was, and it would draw unwanted attention to her. She tied him to a post by slipping a short rope around his neck and gave him a last reassuring pat as she joined the men. She hated being parted from him and felt a tug of anxiety as his pleading eyes vanished from view.

But once inside, she was overwhelmed by colours and sensations. The King's hall was Viking in design, but exotic in detail. Rich smells, not of ale, but of spiced wine, hit her nose alongside the expected aromas of cooked meat and burning wood. They moved through an antechamber, every wall decorated with glittering hangings and carved faces looking menacingly out from beam joints at the strangers in the hall. Passing through a second pair of doors, the King's court appeared in full glory.

It could have been Valhalla, final resting place of gods and heroes itself, Alva thought. The roof was so high that she could barely make out the many writhing beasts and dragons carved into the ceiling. Colour hit her on every side, from the bright enamelled tiles beneath her feet to the embroideries taller than she was, depicting battles of heroes and the ride of Valkyries. Long tables, worn smooth with the arms and elbows of many visitors, stretched the length of the hall, each covered with sparkling cups, flickering lamps, and numerous treasures.

Passing the huge smoking hearth in the centre, upon which a cauldron the size of a small boat hung from a solid chain attached far up in the rafters, they moved closer to the throne. Raised by a series of steps, so he could look down on the activities of the hall, sat a fearsome ruler. Leaning back confidently, King Ragnall passed his hands over the two serpent heads that curled into his fists on the armrests of the enormous wooden chair. He was surrounded by furs, but he wore a patterned tunic the like of which Alva had never seen, with squares of blue, red, and green wool repeating.

His cloak was bound not with a simple brooch like those of the men around her, but with a bejewelled ring the size of Alva's hand. A spear

of solid silver held the brooch in place, piercing the fabric and emerging pointing and deadly across his chest. He was startling to look at. A mass of brown and red hair seemed to explode across his face and down his chest, with crystals and beads woven into his enormous beard. Alva couldn't see his eyes, and she realized this was because he wore a fine silver helmet. Boars and serpents wound over the surface, and it gave Ragnall the impression of being god-like. Alva shrunk in awe before this other-worldly ruler.

'Are you the men of Kilsgard?' He spat the name of their town through his teeth. Did this mean he didn't trust them? His deep voice boomed around the cavernous hall.

There was silence while the men shifted their feet uncomfortably. Eventually Grim spoke up. 'Yes, my lord.'

'I hear from the harbour master that you were driven towards my city by harsh storms on the sea. What do you want here?'

Spluttering slightly, Grim replied, 'Just a little food and lodgings, my lord. We need a day or two to send messengers up the coast to see if the rest of the party we travelled with made it to the destination.'

'And what was your destination?' Ragnall asked, his beard hair flickering in the light of many lamps.

'Lindisfarne, my lord. We were bound there on behalf of our Jarl, Erik of Kilsgard. He was negotiating the return of hostages and treasures to the monks.'

Ragnall leaned forward, seemingly interested. 'What treasures were these?'

Grim floundered for a moment. In the silence, Magnus stepped forward. 'We had relics connected with the great king-saint Oswald. His bones and book. The monks want to see them returned.'

'Monks!' Ragnall boomed, his voice ringing with indignation. 'Don't talk to me about monks. Greedy, grovelling weaklings, who take all and give nothing. It's hard enough to tolerate the priests in this city, but at least they seem to do some actual work. No, the monks had to go. We showed them the true Viking way to deal with books and bones. We turned them to ash.'

He gave a startling laugh, before casting his steel face back on them. Alva saw her uncle's face wrinkle with disdain at this statement and felt a knot in her stomach. The king wouldn't like that reaction. 'You don't agree?' Ragnall boomed at Magnus.

Pausing, Magnus slowly answered, 'I have travelled many lands, my lord. Books are treasured highly by many across the world. If I don't understand what value others place in a thing, I have tried to unravel why they are treated as valuable. I have found books to be precious and interesting.'

The men cast worried looks between them, as Alva shrunk deeper into her cloak. Magnus had dared to disagree with the King! No one spoke, and the silence seemed to last an unbearable time. Finally, Ragnall replied, 'Books might be useful, but monks and bones are not.' Then he looked more closely at Magnus, his eyes travelling to his side and settling on Alva. Her furs were not pulled high enough to hide her face and bright red hair.

'Is that . . .' Ragnall asked, 'a girl there with you?'

The men turned burning glances her way, each of which felt like they seared into Alva's cheeks. No one moved.

'Well?' said Ragnall, moving further to the edge of his throne.

Magnus stepped forward. 'This is my niece, my lord.'

Ragnall gave a low, rumbling chuckle. 'A small shield maiden, hey? I like to see spirit in women. But the gods know I'm regretting that now. The English warrior queen I'm currently battling with is particularly spirited.'

He looked away for a moment, as if chewing on a thought. 'What's your name, girl?'

Alva could hardly breathe, but with a tight chest and clammy hands she managed to whimper, 'Alva.' Catching herself just in time, she tried again, 'Alva Bjornasdottir, my lord.'

Ragnall chuckled low and menacing again. 'Alva Bjornasdottir, hey? Alva, "daughter of Bjorn". I had a man of Kilsgard through here perhaps one winter ago. A good man. A good drinker. I liked him. His name was Bjorn. You wouldn't know him, would you?'

Alva couldn't speak. She was dumbstruck. Magnus came to her rescue. 'My brother, my lord. Bjorn. He was here? That is why my niece has crossed the seas. She is searching for him, foolish and reckless though that journey may be.'

Ragnall stroked his beard while looking

through his metallic eyes at Alva. Shock and fear were turning her to stone. She was sure she would never be able to move from this spot. 'Not entirely foolish, I think. I want to know what became of your father too, girl.' Ragnall gave a sudden stomp of his foot on the floor. It shook Alva from her stupor. 'Fetch me Father Michael at once!'

Servants who had hidden in the shadowy corners of the hall suddenly appeared, and just as suddenly vanished through the wide doors. Ragnall turned again to Alva. 'So, you want to follow your father, do you? Well I hope you don't follow him in treachery. His choices disappointed me greatly. From the hospitality of my hall he went to the skirts of my greatest adversary. A woman no less! The bitter queen of Mercia.'

Leaning back once again, Ragnall seemed to turn from terrifying tyrant to calm leader in one motion.

'I want to know where you people of Kilsgard are at all times. Lodgings will be made available for you within the court buildings. I have a weakling priest who serves me, Father Michael. I've disposed of most of his kind, but have kept him under my control. He has keys to the city, can speak our tongue, and will take care of the arrangements.'

As if summoned by name from the air, a frail old man in tatty priest's garb tottered towards the king. Another figure moved behind him in the shadows. As his face hit the light, Alva saw he was a boy, of roughly the same age as her.

'You summoned me, my lord,' the old man croaked, in the Norse she, the men, and the king spoke. His face was clean-shaven, but the rest of his appearance was unkempt.

'Look what we have here, Father Michael. Do you remember the Viking turncoat who disappeared to the arms of Aethelflaed last year? Here we have his daughter and brother!' Alva bristled with anger as she heard her father spoken of in this way. Her palms were sweaty and she could feel a pulsing panic building up inside her. This was going very badly. Just by being here she had put all the men in danger. And at the very start of her search for her father, it looked like she had already jeopardized everything. She shot a frantic gaze up at Magnus, but he simply stared resolutely ahead.

'I remember Bjorn of Kilsgard, my lord,' the

old priest croaked. 'I thought him a fine man. His defection to the Mercians was a great blow.'

Turning again to Alva and Magnus, Ragnall said, 'You cannot escape my watchful gaze. I will summon all of you here again soon. In the meantime, send messengers after your lost ships, and keep your heads down. If I hear even one mention of the men of Kilsgard I will have you all strung up on Hallow's Hill.' With a loud clap of his hands two armed servants materialized in front of the throne. Their meeting with the king was over, and it could not have turned out worse. Alva felt the strands of the Norns twisting tightly around her, suffocating her, squeezing the hope out of her.

Servants of the Son of Mary

Alva sucked cool air into her lungs as she emerged out of the King's hall. Looking at her companions, she could feel the anger and resentment bubbling among them. Grim rounded on her and Magnus.

'You just couldn't keep your mouths shut, could you? Both of you! All you needed to do was stay out of sight, but no. Magnus, you had to offer up opinions on books. And Alva, you should have stayed hidden. Now look at the situation. We are glorified prisoners. Our runes are cast and we are under the control of that . . .'

He trailed off, aware that the priest was next to them. Two armed guards were drawing closer as well, but the young boy Alva had seen inside the hall had seemingly vanished. Slightly breathless, the priest spoke hastily in Norse, 'Men of Kilsgard. You must follow me. I will prepare your food and lodgings. Come this way.' He gestured for them to follow him, and the disgruntled men trudged reluctantly after him. Alva grabbed Fen from where she'd tied him and dragged him along behind her.

Magnus sidled alongside Grim and whispered to him, 'I will arrange for messengers to travel to Lindisfarne. I'll find a scribe near the church and send the monks details of where we are and what has happened.' Grim gave a final snort as he turned away. Father Michael looked curiously at Magnus, as he and Alva fell to the back of the line.

The priest took them all to a row of small huts a short walk from the hall. The houses were dirty and dilapidated, but at least they would have a roof over their heads. The men trailed in grumpily. Sigurd shot a final glance back at Alva, his blue eyes full of sorrow and concern. The two guards positioned themselves either side of the door. Father Michael, however, clapped his arm across the entrance in front of Alva and Magnus. Gesturing at the guards, he said, 'I'll take these two. They need to write messages and can use my equipment at the church. I presume you CAN write?' he said to Magnus. 'Of course,' her uncle replied tersely. The priest continued speaking with the guards, 'Send someone after us if you wish.' The two guards exchanged a concerned look, then one said, 'Okay, priest. But I'm posting Floki outside your church. Don't think you or those two can go anywhere without us knowing about it!'

Father Michael spun on his heels and began moving quickly down the street. 'Come on!' he called behind him. Surprised, Alva, Magnus, and Fenrir hurried along after the unexpectedly fast old man. They were now alone with the priest. Magnus spoke. 'Father, this is a very unfortunate turn of events. We wanted no drama in your city. We want no trouble with King Ragnall. I just want to write some letters.'

'We cannot talk here,' the priest whispered quietly. 'Follow me.' He shuffled away from them. Alva cried out, 'What about Fen?' The old man cast a disinterested look at Fenrir and said, 'Bring your wolf with you. I'll find him something to eat.'

Fenrir was happy at least, glad to be back

on solid ground and unaffected by what the King had said to them. For him, Jorvik was full of promise, with stolen treats and potential adventures around every corner.

As the King's hall grew smaller behind them, they approached a stone gateway. Alva had been told that giants had spread across the world, lifting huge rocks and raising walls. They must have built this gate and these high defences. They passed under the archway, and saw how moss and the passage of time had eroded some of the stone. Yet she was still amazed that something so ancient could stand so strong.

'It's amazing to see the work of giants,' she said to Magnus, trying to cut the silence between them.

'These stones were not laid by giants,' he replied tersely. 'They were put here by armies of men hundreds of years ago; men who were ruled by an emperor far south in a city called Rome. Really, Alva, do you know nothing?'

The comment stung, but she realized she had a lot to learn if she was to travel to new lands. Musing on these Romans and their high walls, she saw more stone ahead of her. The tall towers of the church Magnus had called 'Minster' were much clearer now. 'Did the Romans build that too?' she asked.

'No,' he answered sternly. 'That was built by Christians. It is still old, but not as old as the walls and gates.'

'We're not going to the Minster just now,' Father Michael said, clearly having listened to their conversation. 'My church is just here.' On a corner of the road, and jutting out at a strange angle, was a building with a huge wooden tower sprouting from its centre. 'I took my name from this church,' he said. 'It is called Saint Michael of the Belfry, because it houses the main bell of the city. I ring it at dawn and at dusk, but at one time it sounded throughout the day and night, to let the monks know when they had to pray.'

Father Michael raised a huge key, which hung from a rope around his waist. He put it in an old lock, and the oak doors parted. 'You keep the churches locked now?' Magnus said inquisitively.

'No church is safe in this city, and neither are the priests and monks,' Father Michael replied. 'If a book, relic, or chalice isn't nailed down, some Norseman will take it as treasure. There are few true God-fearing men left, and even fewer left to guide them. But I've managed to keep my position, mainly because I learnt your Norse tongue. The King can't read or write, and only I can keep him informed of what is happening in the other kingdoms.'

'When I was here some ten winters ago I met many monks who made use of the books in the fine library. What has happened to them?' Magnus asked.

Looking slightly surprised, Father Michael said, 'You are an educated man, then? The monks are dead. The books are burnt. There have been many changes in this city these past few years. Come upstairs and I will tell you more.' As they left the street, Alva just caught sight of an armed guard resting himself against the wall opposite. That must be Floki. They were being watched.

Alva, Magnus, and Fenrir followed the priest through a small dark chapel. It was bare and simple, with just a few faded paintings on the wall. In one image, Alva could see a brave-looking soldier with a sword and huge wings, standing on top of a snake. The priest eyed Alva. 'That's my patron saint, the archangel Michael. He is a fierce warrior, who defeated the devil in the guise of a serpent.'

'He looks just like the hero Sigurd. Except Sigurd didn't have wings,' Alva replied.

Father Michael gave a considered look at her. 'You think the same way as many of the Norse settlers here. Saint Michael can be replaced by Sigurd. Christ on his cross is Odin hanging on the world tree. There are connections, of course, but these pagan ideas cannot entirely wash away the Christian faith here in England.'

He led them towards a second door at the back of the small chapel. Magnus bowed his head as he went through, and they began a sharp ascent up a narrow staircase. Alva was cold, tired, and hungry, but she dragged her exhausted feet up ten, twenty, thirty, forty steps. Eventually the stairs opened on to a wooden cage-like structure. At its centre stood a huge bell, made of solid metal. Alva ran her fingertips over the smooth surface, and as she tapped it she felt the sound vibrate beneath her hand. They were in the bell tower, and looking around Alva gasped at the whole city unfurling beneath her.

'It's an incredible place,' Alva said. 'If I had stayed in Kilsgard I would never have seen such a sight.'

'Well, Jorvik may be the end of our journey at

this rate, Alva,' Magnus said.

The priest went to the far end of the belltower where a table and benches were arranged, settling his weary body down with creaks and cracks. Some came from the furniture, but most came from his old bones. Alva went to sit alongside him, and Fenrir curled up by her feet.

Father Michael took a long look first at Magnus then Alva, as if mulling over a puzzle in his mind, then inhaled a deep breath. 'I'll get you ink and vellum for your letters, Magnus, but first I need some information from you. I think I can trust you, and would like you to help me if you can. You see, I work for the King and appear loyal to him. But I am not blind to his cruelty.'

Magnus joined them at the table. 'Are you sure we are safe to talk here?'

'We are safe as long as we are inside my church,' Father Michael replied. 'Listen to me. I am old. I am tired of watching the city and people I have loved my long life destroyed around me. And I am telling you this now because I also told your father, Alva. It is because of me that Bjorn left Jorvik for Queen Aethelflaed in Mercia, but Ragnall has yet to discover my involvement. And I can tell you what you want to know about your father.'

Diminisher of Falsehoods

Alva couldn't speak. Every hair on her body stood up as if listening for more. She had so many questions racing around her mind, but which to ask the priest first?

She finally settled on, 'When was my father in Jorvik?' Wrinkles appeared around each of Father Michael's eyes as he smiled.

'He arrived here in the spring months, nearly a full year ago now, and was accompanied by a small group of men from Kilsgard. They had goods they wanted to trade with the craftsmen, but Bjorn was intent on more. He went to King Ragnall to ask if he could do some paid work for him, defending his position in the city and fighting for him. Bjorn demonstrated his considerable strength and skills before the King, and they exchanged oaths. He was due to train the men of Jorvik in fighting techniques. He and his men were to be paid handsomely for their efforts.'

'My father wanted to fight FOR King Ragnall?' Alva asked, shocked at the priests' words. 'But he would never give his allegiance to such a nasty, cruel, evil . . .'

'Ragnall can be courteous and civilized when he wants to be. He could see your father was strong and confident, assured of his skills, and ready to make money to take back to you in Kilsgard the best way he knew how.'

Magnus interjected, 'Bjorn had been a mercenary soldier in Constantinople, before he met your mother, Alva. He made an oath to fight for the emperor as a personal bodyguard, and became rich and famous before he was called back to Kilsgard. We had great need of riches so he must have considered this a good way to provide for you, Ivan, and Brianna.'

Father Michael nodded sagely at Magnus, then continued with his story. 'At first Ragnall courted Bjorn, offering him fine wine and plundering him for advice on trade routes and rulers of the South, where the King had not travelled before.

'But he soon felt threatened by the loyalty Bjorn received from the people of Jorvik. He trained men AND women, Christians AND Vikings, binding them together. In the two weeks your father and his men stayed in the city, Ragnall's treatment changed. He toyed with Bjorn, holding back his payments. Your father was unhappy, Alva, as he wanted to be amassing money for you and your mother. He was also talking to the people of Jorvik, hearing tales of Ragnall's cruelty.

'One fateful day in early May, a monk from the abbey dared to cross the King. Furious, the King ordered all the monks dragged to King's Square and a great fire raised into which he threw the ancient works of the famous library. The monks were flogged and expelled from Jorvik, and many of the books were lost forever in the flames. Bjorn could not witness such ignorance and cruelty. I took him from the scene, straight up here to the tower. As I sit with you now, so I sat with him. And what I tell you now, I said to him.'

'You made him an offer?' Magnus asked.

'He wanted money, and he wanted to fight for a just ruler, not one prone to torturing and destroying the people around him. I told him of the Lady of the Mercians.'

'Who is the Lady of the Mercians?' Alva asked, her eyes widening at the thought of a shield maiden with the powers of a king.

'Aethelflaed is a warrior woman unlike any other. Daughter of the great King Alfred of the Anglo-Saxons, she rules her people, her army, and her family with the strength of ten men. She is Ragnall's biggest threat, and the two are preparing for a great battle, which will see one or the other defeated very soon.'

'And my father went to her? Where?' Alva cried.

'Aethelflaed wanted strong warriors too, and men who could tell her what plans Ragnall was making. I wrote to her, giving her information of your father and the men of Kilsgard. She replied immediately, saying they would be given all their desires if they joined her at her court at Tamworth in Mercia. I have a copy of her letter here.'

Father Michael raised his weary body with more clicks and cracks, but as he began to shuffle towards a cupboard in the corner, the sound of fast footsteps came thumping up the staircase. Alva stood up and felt every muscle tense, ready for combat. Fenrir went from fast asleep to growling shield, as he leapt up and put himself between the entrance and Alva. But it was not a helmeted warrior, ready to drag them before the King. Instead, the ruffled brown hair of the boy Alva had seen earlier popped through the gap in the floor. He was out of breath, but called out in Norse, 'Father Michael, I've got the parchment.'

The boy stopped suddenly once he'd leapt up from the stairwell. He looked at Alva, then Magnus, and shifted awkwardly from foot to foot, pushing his hands through his wild dark hair, trying to flatten it down. Alva noticed his fingers were stained black with ink, and dimples pricked each round cheek. His deep brown eyes looked at the ground as he waited for one of the grown-ups to speak.

'This is Alfred,' Father Michael said eventually. 'He was orphaned as a young boy and became my ward. I am teaching him to read, write, and preserve the wisdom of earlier Christians here in Jorvik. He's a good boy most of the time. But I need the eyes of your wolf there to keep up with his antics.'

Alfred looked up momentarily at Alva, and a quick smile lit up his face. Then he took a longer look at his mentor. 'Father,' he said, 'you look tired. You must sit down.'

Alfred put a protective arm around Father Michael, guiding the priest back to the bench. Alfred was taller than Alva, but rather skinny and pale. He had virtually no muscles yet and his back bent over slightly, as if he had spent all his days hunched over a desk. Nervously, Alfred spoke again, 'Why were you up? What can I fetch for you?'

'I want to show them the agreement that was signed between Bjorn and Aethelflaed. Then we can ask them our favour.'

Magnus locked eyes with Alva for a moment. His expression said, 'We agree to nothing. Yet.' Alfred hurried over to the cupboard and pulled out boxes stuffed with parchment. Riffling through, he drew out one page and raced back over to Father Michael. 'Here it is,' he said, unfurling it on the table. He was exhausting to watch, Alva thought. He seemed to rush everywhere, even in this small room.

'What is in this document?' Magnus asked.

The priest passed the parchment to Magnus.

Alva looked over his shoulder, making little sense of the tiny, scrawling handwriting. 'It is in Norse,' Magnus said, surprised.

'Yes,' Michael replied. 'Aethelflaed has a great mind and understands that speaking the language of the Norse settlers ensures a greater bond with those in the North, so she taught herself the language. It is not too different from our tongue,' Father Michael said. 'I have learnt it and so has Alfred. Many here in Jorvik speak both.'

Magnus spoke. 'It's an agreement of payment for military service, and the three men who travelled with Bjorn last year have signed their mark alongside his name.' Alva saw crosses and hatches along the bottom, her father's name signed in full. Bjorn, like Magnus, had learned to read and write while travelling, and was proud he could write his name rather than just put a mark.

'But there's a phrase here I don't understand,' Magnus continued. 'It says, "For the other matter discussed with Father Michael of the Bell Tower, Bjorn will be paid additionally". What other matter?'

Alfred and Father Michael looked at each

other. 'Aethelflaed had asked me to keep watch in Jorvik for Norsemen passing through who were literate, worldly, wise, and had travelled across Christendom. I was to let her know as soon as one arrived in the city, as she had need of such a man for a very specific mission. I know little more than this, but I told her of Bjorn, since he was just such a man. Aethelflaed was to tell him more once the men arrived in Mercia, and I know nothing else than this.'

Alva felt a sinking sensation in her stomach. She knew that Bjorn had travelled to Francia from England, and had told his companion Ingeld of a secret mission. This confirmed her fear that her father had been drawn into something complex and dangerous. Her journey onwards was looking yet more uncertain and challenging.

'It sounds to me like espionage,' Magnus said thoughtfully. 'She wanted him to do something secretive, and something that would take him to the continent. But what do you want from us?'

The priest looked down at the table then spoke, 'I want you to take Queen Aethelflaed a secret document. The men and women of Jorvik do not want battle. They want her as their queen, and all have put their seals on this scroll. She will pay you well, and you may also find out more of where she has sent Bjorn. It is dangerous, as I have no doubt you will be followed. The King would give anything to have a spy inside Aethelflaed's camp. But I assure you: you will not be going for him. You will be going for me, and for Alfred, and for the many people of this city who want to be free of this dreadful ruler. And you will find a woman worth fighting for.

'We have much to discuss, Magnus,' continued the priest. 'I'm sure you want to know more about what's been happening in the city, and you must write your letters, of course. Alfred, why don't you take Alva for a tour of the city?'

'Aren't we being watched by Ragnall's men?' Magnus replied.

'Never mind that,' the priest chuckled. 'Alfred knows every snicket and nook in this place. They can explore unnoticed. Stay in the shadows. Stay out of trouble. And give this girl the adventure she craves.'

Timber-Fast Boat of the Building Plot

While part of her wanted to hear all the details of her uncle's discussion with the old priest, Alva was not going to pass up the offer of being in the fresh air and having an adventure. Plus, Fenrir really needed to stretch his legs after the long voyage. She didn't wait for Alfred to show the way, jumping to her feet, grabbing Fen, and racing for the door.

The three of them descended the dark rickety staircase, but Alfred touched her on the shoulder as they reached the chapel. 'Wait,' he said. 'I need to make sure no one is watching.'

He slowly opened the door and peered out. 'As I thought,' he whispered. 'The King has stationed a guard on the corner of Petergate. We will have to go out a different way.'

He locked the big oak entrance door from the inside before moving to the east end of the tiny church. Bending down in front of a small altar, he began shifting the rushes from the floor.

Alva watched as he heaved up a heavy trapdoor, gesturing for them to join him. 'Can you grab a torch from the bracket up there, please? It's dark down here.' Alva took the flaming torch in one hand and pulled Fen towards the opening with the other.

'Where does it lead?' she asked Alfred.

'The priests from the Minster would use this tunnel to get to and from the belfry if they needed to sound an alarm bell. We will come out inside the great church.'

Alva felt a thrill of excitement surge through her. She would finally get to see inside that towering building her uncle said was the centre of learning in this strange city. She followed Alfred to the trapdoor as he began to climb down some hewn-out steps on the inside of the dark hole. Alva passed a whimpering Fen down to him before following herself. 'Don't forget to close the trapdoor,' Alfred called out. 'We don't want anyone to find our secret passage.'

The hatch closed behind them, and Alva let her eyes slowly adjust to the darkness of the tunnel. It was narrow and damp, with moss clinging to the walls and all manner of unidentifiable matter crunching beneath their feet. Fen had gathered his composure, feeling quite at home as a night beast in the dark. Torch held aloft at the front, Alfred called out, 'Follow me,' and began racing forward at his usual excessive speed, with Fen bounding ahead. Alva tried to keep up, but kept stumbling on dead rats, damp puddles, and unexpected rocks. Alone, in the darkness, she felt as though the walls were starting to close in on her, but she kept moving forward. Her heartbeat was reaching the point where she thought her chest might explode, when she heard Alfred's voice far ahead. 'We're here!'

Alva caught up with Alfred and Fen at a point where the tunnel seemed to end abruptly in a solid wall. 'Here, hold the torch,' Alfred said, as he began to climb up another set of footholds, carved out of the rough earth. Reaching the top, he slipped his fingers into two holes carved into the slab above his head and pushed the slab upwards and to the side. Gingerly, Alfred popped his head of spiky brown hair out and looked around. 'We're okay,' he called back. 'The chapel is empty.'

Pulling his body out of the hole, he reached back for Fenrir, who went like a newborn babe willingly into his arms. He lifted Fen out of the tunnel and then leant back in, taking the torch from Alva and plunging her in to darkness. As Alva took step after step out from the dark and into the light, she blinked. It seemed they had emerged into another tiny room, since on all sides of her she could see walls of stone. But she could no longer see Alfred and Fen.

'This way,' she heard from a gap to her right, and she saw that she could squeeze out of the enclosed space. On emerging, she gasped at the colour all around her. Above, the wooden ceiling had faces picked out in gold, each of which flickered in the light of two great candlesticks. They were placed on a brightly decorated altar, which Alva now realized was where they had emerged.

'Clever, isn't it?' Alfred said, smiling. 'From the front of the altar you would never know there was a concealed space behind. We've been lucky so far, as very few know of the secret tunnel.'

The chapel was twice the size and height

of the one in Saint Michael of the Belfry, and dripping in wealth in comparison. A painting as tall as Alva herself hung above the altar, showing a woman, dressed all in purple, on a throne. In the candlelight, her warm eyes looked like they were alive, staring into Alva's soul. 'This place is . . . breathtaking,' Alva gasped.

'This?' Alfred answered. 'This is just a side chapel dedicated to Mother Mary,' he said, pointing at the impressive woman in the painting. 'Follow me and prepare to be amazed. I'll take you into the main church.' He passed through an arch at the far end. Fenrir stayed close to Alva's heel and walked with her through the stone gateway.

As she entered the main church, her senses felt under assault from every angle. She had stood in some grand spaces, and the King's hall had made her realize how huge and impressive a building could be. But it was nothing compared to this. Stone columns too large to wrap her arms around reached up like a forest of trees beneath a vast wooden roof. She could stand on the shoulders of twenty men and still not touch the delicately painted rafters above. More colours appeared from every angle. An unusual smell hit her nostrils. Seeing her breathing in the scent, Alfred said, 'That's incense. A few brave priests have stayed in the city and gave a small mass this evening. The air is still a bit pungent.'

It was a strange smell, Alva thought. Spicy and heavy in her throat. The whole experience was other-worldly. From far off in the church a single voice sang delicate notes in a strange language. Moving, mesmerized, into the central area, Alva passed through patches of light and shadows. All her senses were singing.

There were sculpted stone boxes along the sides of the church. 'What are those?' she asked.

'Tombs,' Alfred replied. 'The good and great of Jorvik have been laid to rest in the Minster for centuries. There are famous scholars and abbots of the monastery. But also, some Norse lords and ladies. We can't stay for long in here, but if we leave by the south door we will be sure that none of the King's men will follow us. Then we can really start exploring!' Desperate to spend more time in this cavern of mysteries, but keen to discover more, Alva followed behind again.

It wasn't like her to follow another's lead. In Kilsgard she was always the one leading the way, while all the other children followed her.

But Alva liked this boy. He was chaotic and unpredictable, but also funny, and she hadn't felt like laughing much over the last week. Fenrir liked him too, and they needed him if they were to stay safe in this strange city.

Outside the air was fresh and cleared away the fog of the incense. Alva felt a thrill of nerves, searching the open space for armed guards. It was very dark, but Alfred still had the torch with him. His eyes glinting in its flickering flame, he said, 'Now I'm going to show you the proper Jorvik! Let's head down to Coppergate, as that's where we will find your fellow people of the North. It's more fun down there. We'd best avoid the watchman stationed on Petergate,' he continued. 'We'll take the back route.' Alfred walked towards the ruined walls.

'Do you know about the Romans?' he asked as they came close to another large stone gateway.

'My uncle started telling me about them earlier, but I don't know much. We never heard about them in Kilsgard.'

Alfred nodded. 'They stayed here in Jorvik. Back then it was called Eboracum, City of the Yew Tree.' Alva felt a shiver run down her back. In Kilsgard the yew was the tree of death, so that would make this the City of Death.

As they moved further from the old stone walls, the city changed before their eyes into something more recognizable. Here were huts, shops, homes that Alva recognized from Kilsgard. And here were the sights and sounds of a Viking town. As the thrum of the river drew closer, so the houses became more tightly packed together. The familiar sound of Norse rang around the street, while burning wood, stale ale, and meat smells blended with animal and human waste, to make Alva feel like she was coming home.

'Are you hungry?' Alfred asked her. 'I got some coins today and I'm starving! Let's get some good Jorvik food.' He led Alva and Fenrir out a back gate and along a few more narrow alleyways. Even at this late hour, the town was still full of life and energy here, with market stalls set up selling fresh fish from the river and warming broths.

'I feel like *lapskaus*,' he said, dragging Alva over to a stall full of sweet-smelling stew. 'Two please, Estella.' A big-bosomed woman, with round hips and charcoal eyes, began spooning out of a big cauldron into hollowed-out bread loaves.

'All the sailors eat this,' said Alfred.

'What's in it?' Alva asked, looking suspiciously at the thick brown stew.

'Oh, you know, carrots, lamb, onions. And you can eat the bowl at the end!' Alfred said, pulling a hunk of bread from the side of his *lapskaus.* They took their food down to the riverside and sat dangling their legs over the edge of the wharf, watching the longships bobbing up and down in the water. They took turns sharing

chunks of meat with Fenrir, who caught them in mid-air as they tried to make him leap higher and higher for the titbits.

'I could just stow away again on one of those ships,' Alva said, staring out at the river thoughtfully. 'Then I could try and get back to my mother.'

'You can't leave, Alva,' Alfred said sternly. 'You are under my protection, and if I don't return you safe and sound to Father Michael and your uncle tonight, then all hell will come crashing down around me. Plus, you've got important work to do.' He gave her a wink and returned to chewing the last of his stew-soaked loaf.

Alva was tired. She didn't really want to return to the bitter sea. For now, she was content. She had Fenrir; she had Magnus; and, it seemed, she had a new friend. No, for now she would stay in Jorvik. But she was certain that tomorrow would bring new adventures. The Norns were calling out to her, winding their web tighter around her, and drawing her towards fresh dangers.

Bold Enjoyer of the Glory

They wandered slowly back through the dark streets of a sleeping city. 'We don't sleep at the bell tower,' Alfred told her. 'We will go to Father Michael's home, where I'm sure your uncle will also be resting.'

Manoeuvring through more snickets, Alfred brought them to a low doorway close to the huts where the rest of the men of Kilsgard were sleeping. They could see two of the King's men sharing a skin of beer and huddling for warmth around a small fire. 'You'll need to let yourself into the house. I'll go and distract them.' He wandered over to the men and drew some curiosity from his pocket, which the two armed watchmen bent down to examine. Seizing the opportunity, Alva ducked through the doorway and into Father Michael's home. It was small, warm, and welcoming, with beds made up on benches around the sides.

Magnus was sitting at a table near a dying fire. He put his finger to his lips as Alva came in, gesturing to drawn curtains at the far end. 'Father Michael is asleep,' he whispered.

Alva sat down next to him and, for the first time in what seemed like an eternity, it was just the two of them. Magnus put his long, elegant hand over hers, and in that moment she felt their troubles melt away. 'You know you shouldn't have come on the ship, don't you, Alva?' he said. She nodded, full of guilt. 'I've sent letters. One to Lindisfarne to enquire after the other men, and one to your mother. I've told her you are fine and that we have important work to do that may lead us to Bjorn. I don't want her to worry too much. Only you and I know the full truth.'

'Well,' Alva said, looking down at the table, 'I feel I know some of the truth, but certainly not all of it. What more did the priest tell you while I was with Alfred?'

Magnus drew a pile of parchment towards him and began thumbing through. 'He showed me all this correspondence—years of letters! Most have been sent from monks and priests here in Jorvik to the courts of Aethelflaed, Queen of the Mercians, and her brother Edward. They plead continually for rescue. But they get increasingly frantic in tone once Ragnall becomes king.'

'He's dangerous,' Alva said thoughtfully, 'and scary.'

'Yes,' Magnus replied. 'He is certainly worse than I had been led to believe. No wonder Bjorn defected to Aethelflaed. Father Michael has details of how your father and his men snuck out of the city and where they went. But there is no information of what the Queen had in store for them. I think we need to follow their path and perhaps then we can pick up his trail. This evening Father Michael sent a messenger riding at a gallop to Tamworth, telling the court we are on our way and that we bring with us the most important document yet, signed by all the great people of Jorvik. I know you are tired and probably don't want to travel so soon, but what do you think? Should we go south?'

'Well,' Alva said, hesitating, 'we could

simply travel onwards with the rest of the men to Lindisfarne then return to Kilsgard.' She felt a sinking feeling in her stomach. This was the last thing she wanted to do, but she knew she had to be responsible at this point. She had already embroiled her uncle in too much danger, and this was the safest route for them both.

Magnus sat thoughtfully for a moment, stroking a piece of vellum with his fingertips. 'I don't think our fate lies in Kilsgard right now. We have been asked to deliver an important document that could save thousands of lives. We will be paid enough to take us through the next winter and beyond for our efforts. And we will finally find out more about Bjorn's travels. I think we travel onwards, and I think we should leave as soon as possible.'

Alva's heart sang at her uncle's words. This was what she had come here to do! How could she return to her old life in Kilsgard when the world was only just starting to open before her? 'Yes,' she replied confidently. 'We go on. And we go on together.' They locked eyes for a moment, and Magnus's lips parted in a small smile.

* * *

After the best night's sleep Alva had managed in a week, Jorvik slowly woke around them. Animal noises blended with the rumble of carts and the sounds of a city coming to life. A large pounding came from the door. Father Michael began to rise, but Alfred leapt for the door first to save his mentor the effort. Standing in the entrance was a particularly magnificent, stern-looking Viking warrior. 'Haldor,' Father Michael said deferentially, 'do come in. What can we do for you?'

The man strode into the small space, flicked his long cape out behind him, and sat at the table. He lifted his boots up, leaning far back on the bench with an air of ownership. Magnus and Alva stepped forward from the shadows. 'Ah,' Haldor said, seemingly unsurprised. 'So you two are here. I had called on the other men this morning and they said you had taken lodgings with the priest.'

'There wasn't enough room in the cottages, Haldor—' Father Michael began, but he was cut off mid-sentence.

'Listen,' Haldor continued. 'I am head of the army here. My lord, the King, thinks that you and your men of Kilsgard could be useful to us. We want spies to travel into our enemy's territories to discover more about their battle arrangements. You and your fellow Vikings are only alive now at our command, and you owe us your loyalty. The King wants to see you all first thing tomorrow to discuss exactly how you will serve him. Until you deliver the service he requires, none of you will be permitted to leave Jorvik.'

'What exactly do you want us to do?' Magnus asked, a note of incredulity in his voice.

Haldor picked lazily at some nuts that sat on the table in front of him. His arrogance made Alva rage inside. 'You'll all travel south together. You will be stronger as a band of Viking warriors, and you can surely enjoy some raiding along the way. We have news that Aethelflaed is south at her court in Tamworth, but is raising an army to come to Jorvik. She is fresh from victories at Leicester and Derby, and the greedy sow has her heart set on taking all of the North.

You need to get as close to her camp as possible. We need to know where she is stationed, how many troops she has, if they look fit and well-trained, if they have plenty of food and weaponry. You will assist us, and then you can continue on whatever mission you had in mind. We will keep your ship and this girl as hostages, so you must do as you are instructed.'

Alva felt cold, searing panic surge through her veins and turned a horrified gaze towards Magnus. 'Uncle, I don't want to be left here,' she said, terrified.

Magnus simply clenched his fists tightly by his sides as Haldor continued. 'As I said, you'll be called before the King tomorrow. The King will give you the weapons and provisions you need for the mission. We will take the girl as down payment. If any of you defect while away from Jorvik, the girl will be killed. You've got one more evening together, so enjoy your time while you have it. And remember, there are guards surrounding this place. I will see you tomorrow in the King's hall.'

Haldor popped another hazelnut in his mouth then swept out of the hut without a word of parting. The door shuddered in its hinges as it slammed behind him.

'I'm NOT doing it!' Alva shouted suddenly, banging her hand down hard on the table. All the rage that had been building up inside her came flooding out. 'He's a monster! He's not using us, and he's certainly not stopping me from finding my father.'

Magnus put a silencing hand on hers, pointing to the window where the King's men still stood sentinel.

Father Michael cleared his throat and spoke, almost in a whisper. 'Child, do not be afraid. The King has been waiting for just such an opportunity for some time. But we will outfox him. The arrangements are already afoot. You, your uncle and your wolf will be leaving at sundown, and then you can continue your quest to find Bjorn of Kilsgard. For now, however, you must be patient till the sun sets.'

The Highest Mind-Board

Alva was feeling bored, frustrated, and nervous all at the same time. The afternoon was dragging, and the four walls of Father Michael's hut were starting to feel like a prison cell. She wanted to get moving.

Alfred had been in and out of the house, barely sitting still, constantly busy with errands. She wished she could have joined him, but Magnus had stressed how important it was for her to stay out of sight. Her uncle too had ventured over to see the other men of Kilsgard to discuss an escape plan for them so they could all be free of Jorvik before their meeting with the King tomorrow. As darkness began stealing around the room, Alva heard the cheerful voice of Alfred calling out to the guards.

He and Fenrir entered the house with a flurry of limbs and fur. Alva was not sure how she felt about Alfred being out in Jorvik with her Fen, but the poor creature would have gone mad cooped up all day. And she imagined Alfred was getting all sorts of comments and respect, wandering around town with a tame wolf. 'I think I got everything, Father,' Alfred said as an unimaginable number of parcels and bags were drawn out from his seemingly bottomless cloak. The table nearly full, he threw down two daggers in the centre.

'Where did you get those?' Alva asked in astonishment. All the men of Kilsgard had given up their weapons at the King's hall.

'The men are careless when they leave their arms outside the hall,' Alfred replied. 'Fenrir distracted the guards while I slipped two of the smaller swords out of sight. You will need to have something to defend yourselves on the road. Look,' he said, drawing a third out from under a bench. 'I got this one for myself yesterday.' Alva couldn't help but feel impressed at Alfred's cunning.

'And why do YOU need a sword?' Alva asked suspiciously.

'Alfred will travel with you,' Father Michael said. 'You need a guide, someone who knows the landscape, and someone who can speak fluently in Anglo-Saxon.'

'But another person will slow us down,' Alva argued, casting a disapproving gaze at Alfred's skinny legs and bony frame.

'Look, Alva,' Alfred replied. 'I know you think a weak English boy like me could never keep up with a pair of strong, hardy Norse folk like you. But I am quick, and clever. What's more, I've got very little left for me here in Jorvik. With my parents gone, I have just my friends and Father Michael. If I do this I can help the people of my city, and I can help those who have loved and looked after me. I AM going with you, and there's no further discussion.'

'I will miss you, boy,' Father Michael said, passing an old, bent finger under one eye to brush away a tear. 'I know this is dangerous, but your journey is essential. You must take this with you.'

He held up a roll of parchment. 'Here are the pleas and signatures of all the local rulers in and around Jorvik, both Norse and English. They are begging Aethelflaed to come to their defence against King Ragnall. This is their chance to free their city and bring the conflict between North and South, English and Viking, to an end.'

The priest bent his head over the table and began burning a stick of wax, letting the red drops fall on the join in the roll. 'I am sealing it here, in front of you, with the mark of the Archbishop of the city.' Alva saw him lift a metal stamp from a locked drawer and press it into the hot wax. As it rose up, a mark showing two crossed keys appeared as dents in the red roundel.

'No one is to go near this document other than the Queen herself. You must guard it with your lives, and it will protect you.'

'I'll keep it safe,' Alfred said, grabbing the roll.

'No, Alfred,' Father Michael answered. 'I have asked Magnus to deliver it. Together all three of you, and that wolf over there, will take it safely southwards. Show it to the guards on your arrival, and the Queen will know you are friends.'

'But surely Ragnall will have us followed?' Alva asked. 'And if they follow us they will know that we have betrayed him.'

'We will get you out of here in the dead of

night,' Father Michael replied. 'We have friends across the city and across the land. But keep your ears and eyes open for anything on the track behind you.'

As Alfred busied around, preparing food and drink, they discussed the best route to take to Tamworth, places they could overnight, and what to say when they arrived at court. Alfred also brought out clothes, cut in a southern style. 'You can't go into the Queen's court dressed in full Viking garb. You need to look more Saxon on the road.'

Alva looked in disgust at the woollen leggings and plain white shirt Alfred presented to her. 'I'll look like a scruffy English boy!' she spat.

'But at least no one will look twice at a scruffy English boy,' Alfred answered. 'And you'll need to hide your hair. Here, put this on.' He handed her a pale cotton cap. Disgruntled, Alva tied her wild red hair into a knot and pulled the hat on top. Fenrir tilted his head to one side, confused at her changed appearance. 'I'm keeping my own clothes though,' Alva said, pushing her other possessions into one of the bags Father Michael had laid out on the benches.

Father Michael spoke to them again. 'It is a

long way from Jorvik to Aethelflaed's court. You will have to leave the city on foot, but we've arranged for horses a day or so's walk from here. They will speed you up, but you will be more conspicuous on horseback. Once you have the horses you will need to travel fast, as it will still take you about four days. You must not rest or sleep any more than is absolutely necessary. Avoid the main roads, and try to break up your trail. The most important thing is that you stay quiet, stay out of sight, and get inside Aethelflaed's court before Ragnall's men track you down.'

As afternoon turned to evening, Alva, Magnus, and Alfred solidified their plans. Magnus was particularly concerned about the other Kilsgard men. Father Michael had written to the nearby abbey of Sherburn, to ask the monks there to look after the shipload of Kilsgard men. Alfred had then gone to their lodgings and passed on letters, weapons, and final plans to Grim and the others under a cloak of secrecy.

They were to set off on foot as soon as it was dark, via the northern gate where a watchman who supported Father Michael's plans would let them out safely. Once in Sherburn they could travel to Lindisfarne in search of the other longships, or make arrangements to sail back to Norway.

Alva felt a sense of relief at the thought the other Kilsgard men would not be punished because of her and Magnus's mission. But she also felt knotted up with anxiety, as there were so many strands to these plans. If just one thread were to break, they could all be in peril.

Rowing of Wind-Oars

Alfred had been sneaking a bag or two of their possessions over to Saint Michael of the Belfry throughout the day. The guards barely paid any attention to him, as they knew he was always darting about like a dragonfly. As lamps began to spark up inside the houses and the smell of warm suppers spread like a blanket over the streets, it was nearing their time to depart.

Taking nothing more than their cloaks, Alva, Magnus, Father Michael, and Fenrir went to leave the house. Two armed guards immediately closed in on them. 'Where are you going?' one asked gruffly.

'This man needs me to help him write a letter on behalf of the others from his hometown. All my writing implements are at my church in Saint Michael's. Plus, I need to toll the night bell, so I thought we could go together to do both. I don't want to take my eyes off them for one moment.'

Nodding in approval at the old priest's apparent willingness to follow the King's orders, one replied, 'I will go with you and keep guard outside the bell tower. Sven, go to the hall and request two more guards for this site, then join me at the priest's church.' They had banked on this, and as the two guards went in separate directions, the door to the Kilsgard men's lodging was left briefly unwatched. For a short moment only the men had a chance to make their escape.

'We may be some time, I fear,' Father Michael said. 'The Norseman is somewhat literate, but I fear penning a whole letter may be a slow process.'

The guard looked blankly at them, having never written more than a couple of runes in his life. 'It can take all night,' he replied. 'You won't be left unattended and I'll be on watch outside at all times.'

'So be it,' said the priest before setting off at a slow pace down the main street of Petergate.

Pulling the large key from his belt again, Father Michael released the lock and led the way into the church. 'Would you like an ale while you watch?' he called back to the guard.

'I've brought my own,' the guard answered. 'And remember, I'll be waiting out here until you finish your writing.'

Once they were inside, Father Michael locked the solid oak door. Alva immediately spotted Alfred seated in the far corner of the chapel. He had a bag for each of the travellers arranged around his feet, and yet another set of parcels tied up on the altar. 'I got us some food for the first part of the journey,' he said.

'Always thinking about your stomach,' Alva teased.

'You must get going,' Father Michael said. 'I will head up the tower in a moment and ring the bell for dusk. When I do, lift the trapdoor: any noise will be drowned out. Then Alfred can lead you down the tunnel.'

But before the old man could take to the staircase, Alfred flung his wiry arms around him. 'Father,' the boy said tearfully. 'What will happen to you when King Ragnall discovers your betrayal?'

'I am old, boy,' Father Michael replied, taking his hands and looking into his eyes. 'If Jorvik remains trapped under a tyrannous leader, it will be young ones like you that suffer in the future. I've had a rich and long life. I would rather Ragnall took out his revenge on my old bones, rather than on younger ones. Do the best you can, and don't worry about me. My time is nearly up, and this way I can say I did all I could with what I had left.'

Boy and old man shared a long, tearful embrace. Alva felt a pang of guilt that she had never exchanged a proper goodbye with her mother. Then Father Michael began the long climb up the bell tower. Alva and Magnus slung bags on their backs, tucked parcels of food inside their cloaks, and each placed a sword around their waists. Alfred took a torch from the wall and waited.

The bell tolled. Loud, long, strong, the sound shook the tower from the centre outwards. Upon cue, Alfred lifted back the trapdoor with a creak. Finding his footholds, he began to lower himself down. Fenrir followed next, quite calmly as he knew this passage by now. Magnus slipped down after him, and finally it was Alva's turn to enter the tunnel. She took a deep breath and climbed down in to the darkness, closing the trapdoor behind her. Alva kept her eyes on Alfred's torch up ahead, as she made her way through the slimy subterranean passage.

They seemed to have reached the Minster much quicker this time, Alva thought. Alfred again slid the slab aside and the three of them worked to pass bags and wolf through the hole in the floor of the great church. As they emerged inside the chapel, Alfred guided them rapidly through the body of the Minster, and towards the main altar.

Alva knew Magnus had been inside this building before, but she was touched to see his eyes alight as they rested on the magnificent paintings and sculptures again. The group moved behind the great wooden cross that stood some twelve feet high on the large stone altar at the east end of the church. As in the small side chapel, here was another concealed exit, this time a small door that came up only to Alva's waist.

'This is the way into the crawl tunnel,' Alfred said. 'It will take us from the Minster to the Roman walls. There is a gap in the stones where we can climb through without being noticed by any guards at the gates. Once we're on the other side of the walls it will be much safer.'

Alfred took a tiny key from his pocket and unlocked the little door. While she had managed the last tunnel without fear, this one made Alva feel sick. It was barely large enough for her to fit her head and shoulders inside. 'We can't all get through this!' she said.

'Don't worry,' Alfred replied. 'The monks used this tunnel to escape King Ragnall's persecutions and get to safety. Even the fattest of them made it through fine, and it's only a short crawl from here to safety.'

'What about Fenrir?' Alva added, looking down to check he was okay.

'Fenrir is going to be the happiest one in there,' Alfred replied. 'His eyes will work better in the darkness. He's going to be our guide from now on, as we can't take torches any further with us. Wandering around the countryside with great flames in our hands, we would be discovered in moments!'

He gave the wolf a long, encouraging stroke, then moved him towards the opening. 'We need to drag our bags behind us,' Alfred said to the others. 'I'll go in first, and tie mine around my ankle. Alva, you follow me and Fenrir. Magnus, you come last.'

The opening seemed to shrink smaller and smaller the more Alva looked at it. First Fenrir, then Alfred disappeared inside it. She crouched on all fours and began her own crawl. Her heart was palpitating as if it might suddenly give up. The walls felt like they were squeezing her in a press, and stones bit into her kneecaps with every movement she made. Magnus slid in behind her, pulling the small door shut, and complete blackness engulfed them.

This must be what the journey to the afterlife feels like, Alva thought. She could see nothing, but her ears slowly tuned in to the sounds around her. Fenrir gave supportive calls up ahead, while Magnus whispered encouraging words from the darkness behind. Alva began to shiver as the wet ground seeped into her leggings and tracked cold up her body. There was nothing to be done but to keep crawling.

As before, Alfred and Fenrir seemed to move much further and quicker than her. After what seemed an eternity, she heard Alfred congratulating the wolf up ahead. 'Well done, boy! We've made it out.'

There was no trapdoor or stone slab this time. The hole simply emerged beneath the roots of an

old oak tree, perched against the far side of the old Roman wall. She pushed mud and rocks out of her way and finally could stand up straight. Her back clicked painfully, her knees ached, and she was covered in muck. But she was free.

Magnus looked furious as he emerged behind her. 'Surely we could have simply taken our chances at the gate rather than suffer this indignity,' he quietly seethed.

'We had guards waiting for us outside Father Michael's church,' Alfred reminded him. 'And this way we've ensured your fellow Norsemen can make it out of the city without being watched. Surely that's worth a little bit of discomfort?' He shrugged cheekily at Magnus, who rolled his eyes at his overconfidence.

They all stood up and silently brushed dirt from themselves. Alfred pulled plain brown blankets from their bags, and they each warmed themselves by throwing the thick wool over their shoulders. 'Now we must keep out of sight,' Alfred whispered. 'This part of the city is still full of people, and we will navigate through backyards and snickets until we are out on the moors. I'll guide us for now, then Fenrir will take over. Let's go.'

Of the Seaweed of the Hill-Slope

Alva adjusted the cap on her head, covering it with her cloak, so she felt like a spectre creeping through the edges of the city. More huts and houses spread out in front of them, but rather than head for the main road, Alfred wound them past chicken coops, outbuildings, back doors, and rubbish pits. By keeping moving, Alva felt warmth spread through her cold body. There was also a thrill of excitement tingling across her skin, which made her feel flushed and alive. This was true adventure. This was what she had craved back in Kilsgard. Life and death hung in balance, and she had something important that only she could do. This was power.

Somewhere inside her a quiet voice, which

sounded like her mother, ushered a warning. 'Beware of pride, Alva. It will tie you in knots and leave you alone.' But she brushed the thought aside with the pounding rhythm of her feet.

Eventually wooden houses gave way to a wide expanse of woodland. They left the lights of the final few buildings behind them, and the silver glow of the moon was their only torch now. Fenrir was in his element. He pushed his nose delightedly into the leaves and debris of the forest floor, lunged after small creatures, and bounded happily over tree roots. This was the most freedom he had experienced since leaving Kilsgard, and his wide night eyes gazed around happily at his companions.

'Come on, Fenrir,' Alva said, tugging him by the scruff of his neck. 'You've got work to do. You're our guide out of here.'

They came to a vast clearing, where the countryside unfurled like a patterned rug below them. Magnus leant against a tree for a moment, drawing a wooden object from his pouch. It was a small rectangle, with a string set with knots along its length. Magnus took one end of the string between his teeth and pushed the rectangle of wood away from him until the rope was taut. He then held it up to the sky.

'What's that?' Alva asked.

'The Arab explorer I bought this from called it a *kamal*. It will allow us to navigate at night using just the stars. Come here, Alva. I'll show you how it works.'

Standing next to her uncle, she watched him line up the base of the wooden shape with the horizon. 'Can you find Polaris, the North Star?' he said through the string trapped between his teeth.

'It's there!' Alva said, pointing to the brightest star in the sky. Magnus began to draw the wood towards him until the star was blocked. He tied a knot in the string and began furiously scribbling on a wax tablet. 'We could just use Polaris to guide us, but this is far more accurate and will allow us to keep to the right course as night progresses. With Fenrir's eyes, Alfred's speed, your courage, and my calculations, we are a formidable team.'

They set into a steady pace south-east, Polaris shining brightly behind them and Fenrir scanning the safest route ahead, while they placed their feet in each other's steps.

As the moon rose higher in the sky, Alva began to feel tired. Her legs were getting heavier each time she tried to move them. 'Can we take a short rest?' she asked eventually. Magnus looked reluctant to stop but knew he couldn't keep going alone. 'A few moments,' he said.

They threw their bags down and placed their rugs on the ground as blankets. 'Do you think we can light a fire yet, Magnus?' Alfred asked.

'I don't think so,' Magnus replied. 'We are still near to Jorvik and don't want to draw attention to ourselves. Wrap more clothes around you and perhaps have some food. That should keep you going through the night.'

Alfred passed some bread and meat to each of them, throwing a particularly juicy hunk of beef to Fenrir. Fen gobbled it down in one, then came over to Alva. He wound himself around her, covering her cold limbs with his warm, soft fur. Staring at the stars above, the slow breath of her beloved wolf calming her, Alva felt this was one of the best experiences of her life. As they all sat still and silent, a single star shot across the sky.

'A shooting star!' Alfred exclaimed. 'Make a wish!' Alva closed her eyes tightly and her wish became a single floating image in her mind. Her father's face.

Saddle-Beasts

Alva knew they were heading for a specific location: the home of Alfred's aunt. She lived in a village south of Jorvik, and Father Michael had sent a message ahead the day before asking her to prepare horses. Alfred had not seen his Aunt Maud in a few years and was getting more nervous the nearer they got.

'Maud's all right, really,' he gabbled anxiously. 'She's got a fiery temper, but a good heart. She'll help us, I'm sure, as she hates King Ragnall as much as the rest of the kingdom. Just don't say anything to enflame her. We won't stay long . . .'

He continued babbling in this vein as the moon swung over their heads and made for the horizon. Warm pink strands of cloud spread above the trees and billowed over the sky like silks in the breeze. Her body was exhausted, but Alva's heart was alive and joyous. The smells of the forest filled her to the brim, transporting her back to the safe familiarity of Kilsgard.

As the sun was sprinkling the first sparkles of early morning light on the leaves, a small village came into view. 'Is that it?' Magnus asked quietly.

'Yes,' Alfred replied. 'That's Poclintun. My aunt's home is on the outskirts.'

As they approached the village, the forest paths became clearer and wider. Alva felt more exposed and pulled her cloak up higher around her ears. 'Maud's house is south of the village, behind the church, just over there. You stay here. I need to check she's awake and make sure she got Father Michael's message.' He bounded off, and Fenrir gave a little whimper after him.

'Don't worry, Fen, he'll be back,' Alva said, jealously pulling the wolf to her side. He was hers after all.

Dawn was just beginning to change the sky from night to light, but she was already experiencing a growing sense of dread. With sunrise would come news of their escape. She hoped the other men of Kilsgard had made their way safely north and out of the city, and that the guards would take their time checking on Father Michael. A pang of pain shot through her heart at the thought of what would happen to the old priest. She was also worried about their safety on the road. Daylight would make them more exposed, and on horseback too they would find it harder to hide. But they had made their choice now, and she felt she would rather die on the road than return to the rule of Ragnall in Jorvik.

Fenrir busied himself chasing bugs in the tree litter, while Magnus sat down next to her. 'How are you, Alva?' His voice sounded genuine and concerned.

'I'm cold and my feet ache, but I'm okay,' she replied.

'Both your parents would be proud of you right now,' Magnus continued. 'I know you think your father was the adventurer, but your mother faced many challenges before she settled in Kilsgard. She had to choose to leave behind cruel leaders in Ireland and follow a people who were seen by those around her as the enemy. You are having to make a similar choice right now.'

Alva puzzled over his words. She hadn't seen

the similarities before, but she was following her mother's example in some ways. 'My mother chose what felt right in her heart. She didn't blindly bind herself to what she had been raised to trust in, but discovered for herself. I must follow my heart like she did. And my heart tells me we're doing the right thing.'

Magnus nodded sagely. 'The more you see of the world, Alva, the more you will find the line blurred between right and wrong. People move about, taking with them their beliefs, their customs, their language. They blend and meld with the places they settle until it is difficult to determine Viking from Anglo-Saxon, pagan from Christian. We are all growing and changing with every passing moment. And I am by your side. We will be changed by this together.'

He slipped his slim, strong hand into hers and gave it a gentle squeeze. As they sat silently watching the first smoke emerging from chimneys and listening to the morning cockerel sound his alarm call, Alva felt safe.

Alfred bounded back towards them, waving his arms around in excitement. 'Everything is ready!' he called out. 'Maud has two horses, so you and I must ride together, Alva, but she's made hot broth to warm us. Quick, follow me. We can't rest for long in Poclintun. She doesn't speak any Norse, so I'll translate.'

'Don't forget that I know your tongue, Alfred,' Magnus said, 'and Alva has been picking up plenty. It's not that hard to understand. We all come from similar roots, after all.'

Leaving the forest behind, Alfred led them into a small wooden house. The air was heavy with the smell of wool, and on every side were looms and spindles. A round, greying woman, shrouded in layers of clothing, bustled between the hearth and the table, moving cups and pots with the same speed as her nephew.

'Aunty,' Alfred said somewhat timidly in Anglo-Saxon. 'This is Magnus of Kilsgard and his niece, Alva.'

'I don't want to know names,' the woman called over her shoulder in a harsh tone. 'The less I know about you, your friends, and what you are up to, the better. You will have your broth, take your horses, and leave.' Alva sidled up to the steaming cup and wrapped frozen hands around its smooth horn rim. The warmth spread like spiderwebs up her fingers.

Fenrir gave a small whimper from the doorway,

looking longingly at Alva's broth. Maud spun around and let out a screech. 'A wolf!' she screamed. 'A wolf in my house! Quick, Alfred, get the axe.'

'Please be calm, madam,' Magnus said in a stately voice. 'The wolf is tame. He is my niece's pet and will do you no harm.'

But Maud was riled. 'This is all too much,' she was squawking, pacing back and forth between bags of wool. 'First I have to hand over my horses. Then I must provide safe passage for Norse pagans. And now I must tolerate a wolf in my home! No, you have your broth and you leave immediately.'

She stuffed cups into each of their hands and moved them towards the door. 'Leave your cups on the step,' she said, angrily closing the door behind them. A few seconds later the door opened slightly. 'Alfred, once you have finished with this insane mission, you must return to me for lunch one Sabbath.' The door closed sharply again.

Of the Stream of the Land of the Snowdrift of the Earth

Alfred looked embarrassed, while Alva felt bewildered by the noisy barrage of angry Anglo-Saxon. 'I did say she was rather highly strung,' Alfred said apologetically. 'But not to worry. We have all we need. The horses are tied up round the back.'

They weren't the smartest horses Alva had ever seen. One was a tall grey stallion, with white brushes of hair around each hoof and a long fringe that covered his face. The other was a skinny chestnut mare with gentle, almond eyes. They were saddled, with reins and bits ready to go. 'I'll take the stallion,' Magnus said. 'You two will share the mare.' Magnus began tying all the bags to his larger horse. 'What are their names, Alfred?' he asked.

'The boy is Modig, and the girl, Epona,' Alfred replied.

Magnus came near to Alva and began to help her into the saddle. 'Your horse is named after a famous goddess,' he said. 'She will keep you safe.'

Alva felt nervous. Her father had taught her to ride when she was little, but since he had left Kilsgard she had not sat on a horse. Alfred seemed much more confident, jumping into the saddle in front of her. 'I'll ride first,' he said enthusiastically. 'I ran a lot of errands on horseback, both for Father Michael and for the monks of Jorvik. I can ride as well as I can run.'

Alva bridled at having to let this boy take the lead, but she was tired and welcomed the chance to rest a little. 'I'll take over soon though,' she murmured into his back. It felt strange to wrap her arms around his waist, and his hair tickled against her cheek. But as they set off their bodies fell into rhythm, and she drifted into half-sleep to the repetitive sound of the horses' hooves on the damp woodland path.

It felt like only a moment later she was jolted

wide awake at Magnus's call. 'Get behind the trees!' Fenrir, who had stayed close to Epona's heels for many hours now, crouched down in the shrubs and let out a low growl. Magnus jumped from Modig and pulled his horse into deep brush by the side of the path. Alva and Alfred followed him, tapping Epona on the back of her heels so she bent low. Hooves were pounding along the track behind them. Just as Magnus brought Modig to the ground, a group of four horsemen rode past at high speed and churned the path into dust.

Once the sounds had disappeared, Magnus stood up and released the horses from the tight grip he'd placed on their necks. They arose, and Fenrir shook the bristles from his spine, relaxing from his 'fight' pose to something fluffier. 'That was close,' Alfred said, alarmed. 'I couldn't see who the men were, could you?'

'No,' Magnus said, 'but I don't think it can be Ragnall's men on our trail yet. Unless he has sent riders out in every direction. We must be more cautious, avoid bigger roads, and stick to woodland paths whenever possible. Soon we will cross the Hymbra, and after that we will try our luck on the moorland. Come on, we need to pick up the pace.'

Alfred went to take the reins, but Alva said, 'No. I want to ride.' He smiled, handed them to her, and flipped himself up into the saddle. Alva pulled herself up, called for Fenrir, and gave Epona a tap with her shoes. The horse rejoined the road and, encouraged by Alva's words, increased her speed to a fast canter. Trees raced by on either side and soon, as the sun hit the highest point in the sky, they saw a tavern with a small quay outside, sheltered on the edge of a river.

'We've reached the crossing,' Magnus said. 'We'll dismount and enquire about getting a ferry over to the other side.'

Alva nervously dismounted and tucked some strands of hair that had escaped back under her cap. The less noticeable she was, the better. She tied up the horses, and a disgruntled Fenrir too, out of sight.

The three of them walked towards the tavern entrance and crossed under the low beam. In the age-old tradition of watering holes, a young, bright-eyed woman with tumbling brown locks and red lips stood behind the counter cleaning cups, while a sequence of tired, dirty older men

were propped on a bench opposite. All stopped and looked at the newcomers.

Magnus ignored them all and made for a bench in the corner, while Alfred hurried to the counter, exchanging pleasantries in Anglo-Saxon with the young lady. The men continued to stare with burning glances into the back of Alva's head until Alfred eventually returned with three large cups of ale. 'Margaret's going to bring us some bread and soup,' he said happily. 'And I asked about the ferry. Apparently that large chap at the far end is the ferryman, and he will take us and the horses across for three pennies.'

'That seems a lot,' Magnus replied, but he remembered that Father Michael had provided them with a purse of coins to help them reach Tamworth safely. 'Tell him we would like to cross as soon as we've eaten.' Alfred scurried over to the fierce-eyed, bald-headed man, just as the tavern owner, Margaret, thrust three bowls down on the table. As she turned, she took a second look at Alva. A small crease appeared in her brow, but after an uncomfortable pause she turned and left. The soup was thick and sour. Alva had no idea what the lumps were, but each tasted rotten. Nevertheless, they ate quickly, trying to avoid making eye contact with any of the other men in the tavern.

They stood and began collecting their bags when one man drunkenly stumbled over to Magnus. 'That your boy there, eh?' he said in drawling Anglo-Saxon.

Magnus tried to ignore him and pushed past towards the door. 'What's the matter, eh? Don't want to speak with us? Your boy there has no trouble.' He turned to the others in the tavern and raised his voice. 'Seems this fellow is too important to speak with us. Or perhaps he can't speak to us. Perhaps he's not from round here?'

Magnus ushered Alva and Alfred from the building, placing his hand on his sword hilt. In his finest Anglo-Saxon he called back, 'Thank you for the hospitality,' then left the tavern with a slam of the small oak door.

'We've got to get across on the ferry,' he said as they made for their horses. The ferryman was already pulling in the ropes ready for them to cross. Alfred led Epona and Modig on to the flat-bottomed boat, then Magnus followed. Alva had just brought Fenrir to the bank when the ferryman spotted him. 'What's that? A wolf?'

he shouted. 'I'm not taking a wolf on here!' He began to push away from the shore.

Magnus rounded on him, again putting his fist threateningly on his sword. 'We must travel with the wolf. I will pay you extra for it.' He drew a golden coin from his purse and waved it in front of the man. The man seemed nervous but dug his rudder into the mud to stop the ferry drifting out any further. 'That thing comes nowhere near me, or I'll cut its head off with one swing.' He drew his own sword from its scabbard and held it tight in front of him.

The boat was some distance from the shore, but the ferryman looked in no mood to return to the bank. 'Alva, you'll have to jump,' Alfred called out.

'What about Fen?' she shouted back.

'Throw him to me,' Magnus said. Alva had never thrown Fenrir before, and she thought this was not something the proud wolf would be too keen on.

'Leave it to me,' Alfred said, moving Magnus aside. He looked Fenrir in the eyes, slapped his thighs, and called out, 'Fen, come here, Fen!' The wolf looked first at Alva, then at Alfred, before leaping straight into the boy's waiting arms. As Alfred congratulated him with hugs and kind words, Alva leapt after him and hit the boat with a bang. Getting up as confidently as she could manage, she shot an angry glance at Alfred. 'He's not your wolf!' she said stingingly, and she pulled Fenrir away with some force.

They sat in silence as the ferry made the short journey across the water. The ferryman didn't take his eyes off Fenrir the whole time and kept the point of his blade trained on the wolf. When they bumped against the opposite shore, horses, humans, and wolf dismounted without a word, but once the ferry had gone out of earshot, Magnus spoke. 'We are in trouble,' he said. 'We need to stay out of sight in case we are followed. Now if someone asks if two youngsters, a man, and a wolf came this way, the ferryman could give them our exact location. I know the next part of our journey will be long and tiring, but I don't think we can risk taking food or shelter again.'

Alfred rummaged around in one of the bags. 'We've probably got just enough food to get us to Tamworth if we move fast and eat little,' he said. 'We can't give any more scraps to you, I'm afraid, Fen. You'll have to hunt for your supper.'

'It's going to get cold though, Uncle,' Alva said. 'Where will we sleep?'

'We will have the stars as our blanket,' Magnus replied. 'Spring is here, the weather is mild, and we have plenty of clothes for warmth.'

Alva looked at the ground sorrowfully, thinking of her warm, soft bed, warmed by her mother's welcoming hearth, back in Kilsgard. 'Alva,' Magnus said, touching her on the shoulder. 'You wanted adventure. Well, this is a real adventure.'

Hall of the Sun's Stronghold

Over the next few days, Alva, Alfred and Magnus settled into an unusual routine. They would ride fastest and hardest from the first glimmers of the sun's light, until the fields and roads were awake and bustling. Then they would find a secluded spot buried within dense trees, or hidden beneath craggy rocks, and take it in turns to nap. They would ride more slowly and quietly from midday to dusk, avoiding the roads and villages, before picking up speed as the sun began its slow descent. Then they would ride like the wind until they could no longer see the path in front of them.

Alva was finding the process painful. She hated having to rise just as she was dropping into deep dreams. After rain on the third day, her cloak was still damp, and it was difficult to find dry spots to rest. What's more, she had terrible saddle-sore on her backside and leather burns on her hands from gripping the reins. There were few opportunities to talk with Alfred and Magnus, since they all stayed as silent as possible on the road, and would be resting or sleeping while one remained on watch.

But they had managed a few memorable moments together. When the rain came as night was setting somewhere Magnus described as 'The Peaks', they built a shelter. It was wet and laborious, but to warm their soaked clothes Magnus allowed them to light a small fire for a short while. As they watched steam rise from their garments, shrouded in nothing but their cloaks and underwear, Alfred started telling elaborate riddles to keep their spirits up. Each ended with the phrase 'say what I am', and the solutions ranged from handwritten manuscripts to onions. They had laughed as loudly as was safe, and had shared the last of the dried meats and ale. It would be stale bread and river water from now on.

They kept changing their path from Jorvik to

Tamworth, zigzagging back and forth, avoiding the main old roads of Ermine Street and Fosse Way for long stretches to stay hidden. On the morning of the sixth day, they skirted around a small village with an ancient church at its centre. 'That is Stone,' Alfred told them. 'It's famous because of what happened to two royal princes there.' Alva had found his stories of the legends peppering the Anglo-Saxon world fascinating and wanted to know more.

'It's said that the pagan King Wulfhere had two sons, Wulfad and Ruffin. The boys had gone into that forest on the trail of a white stag. There they met a famous saint, Chad, Bishop of the Mercians. He converted them to Christianity, but their father was incensed by their abandonment of pagan practices, so murdered them in cold blood. Their grieving mother brought heavy stones one after the other to that place and built a cairn over her sons' bodies. It was from these stones that the church of Stone was founded. So, Alva, if you see a white stag, don't go following it into the woods, okay?' He gave her a grin.

'If we're at Stone, that means we are only a day's ride from Tamworth,' Magnus responded. 'We must aim south-east, and soon we will see the walls of the royal city.'

By the evening of the sixth day, after seeing virtually no one across deserted marshes and empty forests, the paths were now teeming with people. Alfred told them of the great Mercians who had ruled this place: Penda, brutal pagan king and fierce warrior on the battlefield; Offa, friend of the Emperor Charlemagne and creator of a huge earthwork that still protected the western edge of the kingdom; and now Aethelflaed, greatest of generals, supreme diplomat, saviour of cities, and warrior woman.

It was this 'Lady of the Mercians' who had brought the great royal city of Tamworth back to life after raiding Vikings had destroyed its ancient buildings. She had a huge enclosure built around the perimeter, and a new palace erected that would become the heart of her kingdom once again. Alfred regaled them with stories of her triumphs.

'She was married to an old lord when she was still very young. He was ruler of Mercia, but as he became old and frail she took over all his work with the full support of the kingdom. Some say she is the real Queen of the English, even though she allows her brother Edward to play at being

King. Just a few years ago she led the men of Mercia in a blistering defeat of the Danish men at Tettenhall. I heard that she climbed off the battlefield, bloodied and bruised, bearing the swords of three Viking kings in her hands! She sounds amazing, doesn't she?'

As the wooden walls of the town came into view, Magnus pulled the horses to a stand. 'We cannot enter Tamworth tonight. We need to get clean and respectable before we present ourselves at the gates. Father Michael told me there was a home on the south side of the city where lodging and food would be available to travellers. I am to ask for Edwin, and he will give us a place to rest. He is sympathetic to the people of the North and speaks our tongue.'

'Is it safe though?' Alva asked nervously. 'We are so close to the court and I'm sure the great Lady won't mind if we are a little rough-looking. We've been on a secret mission for her, after all? I'd rather just get inside the walls and into safety.'

'We have to be very careful when we approach the guards at the gates, Alva,' Magnus replied. 'We are going to be treated with suspicion, and they may even think we are acting as spies. We cannot arrive in the depth of night when the Queen will be sleeping. We rest, and then we go first thing.'

Uncertain, but desperate for a warm bowl of food in her belly, Alva followed her uncle's horse around the perimeter of the town. The wooden walls were huge, and she could see nightwatchmen carrying torches parading up and down the ramparts. As promised, there was a welcoming building about five hundred paces from the south gate. Its doors were wide open, and the sound of revelling, songs, and raised voices carried out on to the street. They tied Modig and Epona round the back, alongside a handful of other horses. The hungry animals gladly dipped their heads into a trough full of fresh hay as Magnus pulled the bags from Modig's saddle.

'Stay close to me in here,' he murmured. 'Our last visit to a tavern didn't go too well, and this is a town that is brimming with suspicion of all travellers from the northern kingdoms. War is imminent, and we are potential threats. Stay close, and stay silent.'

Again, Alva nervously tucked her bright red hair under her very grubby cap and left Fenrir resting with the horses. He was exhausted and simply collapsed in a heap by Epona's heels. The other horses barely reacted to the sight of a wild beast and went on munching their food as he fell swiftly to sleep. Alva rubbed his warm fur and made sure he was safe before following Magnus and Alfred to the entrance.

Alva was surprised by the sight that met her eyes inside. It was a throng of people crammed in together, with russet-haired young ladies sitting on the laps of a handful of well-armed soldiers. 'The army has just returned from battles in the Danelaw,' Alfred mumbled to her. 'They're having a little celebration.'

Magnus wound through the noisy crowd, who were too busy telling loud tales of their exploits on the battlefield to pay them much attention. A small, hunched man was sitting near the hearth. 'Are you Edwin?' Magnus asked him in Anglo-Saxon. 'Father Michael said we could find a bed and some warm food here. Is that right?'

The little man turned bright, cheerful eyes towards them, replying in fluent Norse. 'You are welcome as friends,' he said. 'I heard you were coming and want to help you in any way I can.' He began to fuss over them, removing their cloaks and hanging these near the smouldering fire. 'You must be so tired and hungry after your journey,' he went on kindly. 'I haven't much I can offer you, but how does a hunk of warm mutton, carrots, and bread sound to you? And my ale is strong and tasty.'

Alva could have cried with relief at the tantalizing sound of these words. 'Please! Please, yes,' she said abruptly. Edwin gave a hearty chuckle at her words. 'Father Michael told me of this one. You must be Alva? Dear girl, take off your damp shoes, rest your feet on the rugs, and I will fetch you blankets, food, and drink.'

Alva felt safe for the first time in days. As she lowered herself on to the soft rugs, the aches in her back slowly subsided. Alfred reclined next to her, soaking his skin with the warm glow of the fire. Only Magnus stayed alert. But when Edwin placed bowls of aromatic mutton in front of them, even her uncle threw himself wholeheartedly into savouring the taste of hot, delicious food.

The soldiers eventually began to depart, groaning about early morning training sessions and reporting for duty. Soon the building was calm and quiet. Edwin took the opportunity to join them by the fire. 'You've had a long journey,' he said sympathetically. 'But I am glad you are here to help our Lady against that tyrannical pirate Ragnall. You must tell me all about your travels and news of Jorvik.' Full, content, and comfortably confident with two large mugs of ale inside them, all three spoke of where they had been this past week. Magnus was careful not to say too much of Ragnall and his court, but Alfred's lips had become loose.

'And we have very important documents we need to deliver to the Lady of the Mercians,' he slurred. 'We have so much to tell her of the crimes taking place daily in Jorvik . . .'

'Jorvik?' A new voice had entered the room and brought with it a gust of night-time air. 'I can tell you of Jorvik, since I've just left it myself.'

Alva was stunned still. She knew this voice. She knew the man standing in front of her, blond hair surrounding his youthful face like a mane, teeth glinting in the broadest of smiles. She leapt from the floor and into his embrace. 'Sigurd!' she shouted with excitement. 'What has that god of mischief Loki conspired to bring you here? I can't believe it!'

Alfred clambered up and ran to welcome the tall, strong man of Kilsgard. But Magnus held back. 'I came after you, Alva,' Sigurd replied. 'The other men left the city bound north for Lindisfarne, but I did not want to leave you without the help of your townsfolk. I knew you were bound for Tamworth, and I also wanted to see the court of this renowned warrior woman. I hear she has a beautiful daughter who is yet to be married, and thought she might like to bind herself to a strong, handsome Norseman like me.' His bright blue eyes winked conspiratorially at Alva.

The atmosphere was shattered most suddenly, however, by Magnus, who leapt to his feet and in the blink of an eye had his dagger pointed at Sigurd's neck. 'Liar!' he whispered into Sigurd's face. 'You lie. Why have you followed us? Did Ragnall send you?'

Sigurd let out a horrified gasp then said, 'N . . . no! No, Magnus! I have come here to help you! As you know, my father was one of Bjorn's companions when he left Kilsgard last year, and is one of the three men who is yet to return. Like you I want to know what happened to them. I am on the same quest as you. And I want to help you.' They all stood rooted to the spot and Magnus silently scrutinized Sigurd's face. Finally, he lowered the blade and slumped back on the bench.

Sensing a release in the atmosphere, Edwin jumped up and fetched food and ale for Sigurd, while Alva led him over to the fire. He looked frozen to the bone and shaken by Magnus's actions, but he soon began to thaw. 'I did wonder if, like Alva, you were on this latest sea voyage to discover more of your father's whereabouts,' Magnus said. 'Ulf was one of Bjorn's most trusted allies, and it seems he followed my brother down to the court of this Lady of the Mercians.'

'I just want to know where he is,' Sigurd replied pensively. 'Like you, I cannot rest until I know more. Alva, I know you feel the same way.' His crystal-clear eyes looked for empathy from Alva.

She returned his gaze and said, 'Not for one day have I stopped thinking of where my father is. No wonder you want to hear what the Queen has to say.'

They settled into a comfortable camaraderie

around the hearth as Edwin provided anything they wished for. Magnus remained quiet, however, eventually saying that he and Alva should get some much-needed rest. 'Sigurd,' he said, 'I will bring you within the walls of Tamworth tomorrow, but then Alva and I will go alone to meet the Queen.' With this he grabbed Alva's hand and they followed Edwin to a separate room behind the main hall, which had soft furs and woollen sheets laid out. Alva sunk without thinking into the deepest of sleeps. But her dreams were dark. The faces of her father and mother swam in between those of the Norns, but another face slipped between them all. A woman's face—kind, strong, bold—topped with a glittering crown. And through these faces Alva could hear a piercing sound. She could hear a high-pitched, blood-curdling scream.

Beautifully Dressed Oak of Riches

Alva opened her eyes to find Edwin's mouse-like face pressed up close to hers. 'Brought you something to drink,' he whispered, pushing a warm cup towards her. She leapt backwards like a cornered cat, disorientated after her long sleep, unsure for a moment where she was.

'It's okay,' Edwin said gently. 'You have slept like the giants! It's already late morning and your uncle has been pacing around since the crack of dawn. He wanted to wake you, but I told him to let you sleep. You need your strength if you are to meet the Lady of the Mercians!'

He left the cup by her side and edged slowly out of the room. Alva sat up and stretched. That was the most she had slept in many weeks, and her limbs felt more exhausted than ever, as if the many days of tiredness were working their way through her body. She threw her cloak around her shoulders and was delighted to find it was dry and clean. A fresh branch of the river ran close behind the building, and Edwin had given her clothes a scrub, leaving them to warm by the fire. They felt so comforting against her skin, and she suddenly wanted to stay in this small room, to hide from the world, and to give up any dreams of adventure. Being on an adventure seemed to involve being cold, damp, and scared.

She reached out for Fenrir automatically, but when her arms met empty space she remembered that he was outside. Leaping to her feet, she tied on her shoes and ran immediately for the back door. She searched amongst the hooves of the horses and felt a sinking feeling as the hay revealed no wolf. Where was he? Heart pulsing and tears rising in her eyes, she ran back around the front of the house and burst through the main doors. 'Where's Fen?'.

And there he was, curled up by Alfred's feet near the fire, gently taking small chunks of meat from the boy's fingers. 'You're awake!' Alfred said happily. Alva ran to Fenrir and fell by his side.

Rounding on Alfred, she yelled, 'Why have YOU got my wolf? How dare you take him while I was sleeping!'

'He was scratching at the door this morning and Edwin said it was okay to let him in to get warm. We were all letting you sleep,' Alfred replied defensively.

Alva felt the prickles of jealousy across her skin, but Fenrir gave her face a huge swipe with his wet tongue, and she relaxed her limbs. Her fight wasn't with Alfred. She had more important things to worry about today. As if on cue, Magnus sat down beside her.

'You need to wash your face, hair, and hands, Alva. We all stink of the road, and cannot meet Aethelflaed without a good wash. Then put on your best clothes from home. You can wear that wolf brooch your mother gave you. You need to look like a truly fearsome shield maiden today.' Alva saw that Magnus had made an effort. He had braided new beads into his beard, had painted blue woad patterns on his hands and face, and had tied his finest red cloak with a huge silver brooch. She had only seen it a few times before, as Magnus wore it rarely, but she was mesmerized by the swirling serpents that writhed over its surface. He looked formidable; he looked like a Viking.

'Wouldn't it be better if we tried to pass as Anglo-Saxon?' Alva asked.

'Not now, Alva,' he replied. 'Now we present ourselves as the proud relatives of that prized mercenary Bjorn. Father Michael has been in touch with Aethelflaed. She knows why we are here and what news we bring. She is a diplomat, and what she wants more than anything right now is to draw the people of the Danelaw to her in loyalty. The more Viking we look today, the better.'

A creak in the corner of the room reminded Alva of their newest companion. Sigurd stood up, and she could see that he too was in his finest wear. Dragon-headed brooches pinned a fine cloak to his shoulders, and he had combed his hair into thin braids that wound over his scalp as if they were alive and wriggling. He looked terrifying and magnificent. 'Are we ready to go?' he asked.

'You heard me last night, Sigurd,' Magnus answered. 'We will go together inside the walls of the town, but from there just Alva and I go forward.' Sigurd nodded compliantly. 'Now hurry up, girl,' Magnus continued. 'We're all waiting on you!'

She made her hair as tidy as she could manage and pinned her fur-lined cloak together with the brooch her mother had given her. At its centre was a silver wolf's head, which was linked to two silver discs that held her cloak to her shoulders by a long string of bone beads. She painted blue swirls and patterns on her face and arms, carefully drawing a ringed serpent around her left eye. With her sword slung at her waist and Fenrir by her side, she thought she cut a pretty impressive figure. Just as they were about to leave Edwin's home, Sigurd appeared beside her.

'Alva,' he said quietly, 'I want you to know I am your friend and ally. I want the same as you. So that you are sure I am loyal, I wanted to give you back this.' He handed her a piece of fabric the size of her hand. Unwrapping it, she saw her sunstone, glinting in the light of the fire. 'Grim was going to take it north with him and the men, but I knew it belonged to you so snuck it out of his bag. It should help you with your onward journeys.'

Alva held the stone still in her hand for a

moment, delighted to be reunited with her precious treasure. She had one stone and her father had the other. As long as she had it, she felt closer to him. She gave Sigurd a grateful smile and slid it carefully inside her pouch.

'Right, let's go!' Magnus pronounced from the doorway. They said warm goodbyes to Edwin, and Magnus filled his palm with coins from Father Michael as their host threw kind arms around each of them. Falling into line, they began the short walk towards the heavily fortified southern gates of Tamworth. The eyes of soldiers, staring down from the thick wooden walls, tracked their steps. As they approached the enormous bolted doors, two heavily armed men came forward.

'Why do Norse folk approach the city?' one asked in a lofty voice.

'I am Magnus of Kilsgard, and this is my niece Alva. We are here on behalf of the people of Jorvik, and we have a letter sealed with the Archbishop's insignia for Lady Aethelflaed of the Mercians. Please tell her we have arrived.'

The men looked at them suspiciously, but one disappeared back through the gates. While they waited, Alva looked at the people moving in and out of Tamworth. Cartloads of hay were dragged by tired horses, smart men in bright, fitted clothes, adorned with gemstones, moved serenely past the soldiers, and a stream of monks, cloaked in black habits, walked heads down towards the heart of the city. This was a place that hummed with excitement, that seemed poised on the brink of action, that seemed crammed with promise.

Eventually the soldier returned and nodded at the group. They filed through behind him into a street bustling with people. Here the soldier addressed them. 'You must move immediately towards the palace. At the doors, you must show your documents, and you will be given notice of when the Queen can see you. The wolf cannot go into the city. He must stay out here. Go there forthwith.'

He pointed along the road to where it widened around a large timber hall. The outside of the building was painted in bright colours, and the square around it was wide, surrounded with stalls and shops, bustling with people and humming with noise. They all looked at each other, then Alfred spoke. 'I'll stay at Edwin's with Fenrir. I will see if I can leave him there and follow you in later. It should be easier for me to enter as I'm an Anglo-Saxon.' Giving Alfred a grateful look and Fenrir a final hug, Alva followed Magnus and Sigurd, and the three Norse folk strode purposefully towards the hall.

Magnus drew the scroll with the Archbishop's seal from his bag. Different armed men approached, and he raised the piece of vellum. He said, 'We are here on behalf of the people of Jorvik and wish to speak privately with Queen Aethelflaed.'

The men parted, and the three of them walked into an antechamber in the great palace. There were benches arranged along the sides and ten or so people sat perched on them looking tired and bored. 'Wait here,' one of the men said as they sat down together.

Alva leaned back against the wall, readying herself for a long wait. But though they had arrived last, it was her uncle's name that was called next as a guard opened the secure inner doors. 'Magnus of Kilsgard!' he announced. Alva and Sigurd both rose to follow him, but Magnus pulled his niece behind him. 'Stay here,' he murmured to Sigurd, who slumped back down on to the bench.

Alva checked her cloak and beads as she walked into the grand hall. Unlike Ragnall's in Jorvik, this room was huge and largely empty. There were tapestries hanging on every wall, but most depicted Christ, Mary, the saints, and angels. Tall candelabras lit the room with a dance of flames. With no benches, hearth, or furniture to block their view of the far end, Alva's gaze settled solely on a magnificent woman who seemed almost to hover above a glinting throne.

Gemstones were set into the wood of the seat, and it was gilded on all sides. The Queen's wide skirts were also woven with gold, and the effect of all this brightness flickering in candle flames mesmerized Alva. Forgetting her manners, she continued to stare at Aethelflaed, when Magnus had already bowed down in front of the railing which kept the Queen at a safe distance. He looked at Alva angrily and she checked herself, bowing low immediately. They waited in silence for the lady to speak.

'You are Bjorn of Kilsgard's relatives,' she said finally, in a voice that felt like honeyed lemon—sweet and smooth, with a sharp power underneath.

'We are, my lady,' Magnus replied. 'I am his

brother, Magnus, and this is his daughter Alva.'

Aethelflaed rose slowly from her throne and, stepping down from the dais, moved towards them both. Without stopping, she came straight for Alva, taking her chin in long, cold fingers, and pulling her face close. Her green eyes were shaped like a cat's, and her proud face was a perfect heart, framed with harvest-brown hair and topped with a crown of gold. She looked into Alva's eyes. She looked into Alva's soul. Time stood still.

Eventually she spoke. 'Yes. You are Bjorn's girl. But such wild red hair! Is that from your mother?'

Alva spoke with as much confidence as she could muster. 'My mother was a princess from the Dal Raita region of Ireland, my lady.' She felt pleased she had remembered to use 'my lady' this time.

'Indeed?' Aethelflaed stood tall again and smiled. 'You have the spirit of a shield maiden from your father, and the heart of a princess from your mother. What an interesting child you must be. And you, sir,' she said turning to Magnus. 'Bjorn told me all about you. It is you who can read, write, knows Latin, and can speak our English like a native. Is that right?'

'My brother does me too high an honour, my lady,' Magnus said politely.

'And you have travelled, been to many lands, and met with scholars, scientists, astrologers too, he said,' Aethelflaed continued. 'A fascinating man like Bjorn was sure to have equally fascinating relatives. You are very welcome here, particularly as I know you bring me important news from my dear friend Father Michael in Jorvik. Please, pass me the document.'

Alva watched as Magnus passed her the scroll of vellum. She checked the seal then broke it, unrolled it, and read quickly. 'This is good,' the Queen said slowly. 'The great families of Jorvik, English and Norse, all ask me to help them remove the tyrant Ragnall from the city. This is what I have waited for. We have taken the other major cities of the Five Boroughs of the Danelaw, but Jorvik would be the crowning jewel. With this letter I can make plans, raise the army, and take the city back for my brother, the King. I am so very grateful to you both. You have travelled far in great danger to bring this to me. I will of course pay you handsomely for your trouble, but is there anything else I can do for you in return?'

'Nothing, my lady. . .' Magnus began. But Alva felt her pulse quicken and her palms grow sweaty. Without thinking through what she was going to say, she blurted out suddenly, 'There is ONE thing you could do.'

Magnus turned on her abruptly, but the Queen raised a hand to silence him. 'Shhh. I want to hear what Alva asks of me.'

Alva cleared her throat and shuffled her feet nervously. 'It's just . . .' She tried again. 'It's just that I've travelled all this way—by ship, by foot, by horse—all because I want to know what has happened to my father. I want to know why he is still away, and I want to know if he is still alive. Is there anything you can do to help me?'

Aethelflaed walked back over to her and crouched down. Making eye contact, she said in a gentle voice, 'I had something special I needed him to do. It was something my father, Great Alfred, had attempted. And where he had failed, I wanted to succeed. I sent him to look for a very important object, and that is why he is still away.'

Magnus came over to the Queen, saying, 'Was he your mercenary?'

'More than a mercenary,' Aethelflaed said. 'I was to pay him huge amounts of money. More money than he could have earned in a lifetime of raiding. He was given a third when he agreed to the work and was to get the other two-thirds when he returned. However, I will pass onethird to you, his family, since I am sure he would want you to be recompensed for his absence over this time.'

Alva felt a thrill of excitement ring through her bones. Like her father and her uncle, she had a love, or rather a deep-seated craving, for gold and treasure. Aethelflaed was telling her she was to be rich!

'Do you know if my father is alive?' Alva asked. 'And what about the men who travelled with him—Ulf and Leif?'

'I am sure Bjorn is still alive, but I am not sure exactly where he is,' Aethelflaed replied. 'As for his companions, I had news from Francia that they had been killed. Two of the men he travelled with—Ulf and Leif—were murdered in their beds, and the third—Ingeld—vanished. But Bjorn was alive.' Alva felt a searing guilt rush through her. She was delighted to know her father was safe, but poor Sigurd would have to be told about Ulf. He would be devastated.

'Alva,' Aethelflaed said warmly, 'I want you to know more. But as you have seen, there are many waiting to speak with me. Come to the feast I am holding at sundown. We can talk then.'

She gave a long, kind smile. Alva, still captivated, didn't realize that they were being gracefully dismissed. But she saw her uncle turn to leave and followed hurriedly after him.

Outside the hall, Alva asked her uncle, 'What does all this mean for us? Surely we will have to find out where my father is and travel to him?'

'Alva,' Magnus said. 'Your father may be anywhere right now. You're just a young girl. How are you going to follow him?'

'I'll have Fen,' she replied. 'And you.'

'I don't know what is in store for me next. If the Queen is true to her word and gives us half of what she was to pay your father, then we will need to return to Kilsgard with such riches. We should both go. There is little point following your father who-knows-where.'

Sigurd had risen when he saw them and was listening intently to their conversation. 'So she told you more about Bjorn! He's alive. The gods be praised. What about my father?'

They both stared at him, remembering what Aethelflaed had said. Magnus put a gentle hand on Sigurd's shoulder. 'The men went to the continent together on a mission for the Queen,' he said. 'She had news that the others who travelled with Bjorn died in Francia. My heart goes out to you, Sigurd.'

Sigurd went pale, staggered a little, then fell back on to one of the benches. Alva put her arms around him and whispered, 'I'm so sorry.'

But Alva's words of comfort fell on deaf ears. Sigurd's eyes, which were usually so full of life, turned hard and cruel as he muttered, 'That enthroned monster in there sent my father to his death, it seems.'

Wiping a tear from his eye, he turned fast on his heels and raced from the hall.

People of the Moon's Path

Outside the hall, Alva was reluctant to go straight back to Edwin's. Now within the walls of Tamworth, she wanted to explore. 'You go back if you like, Uncle,' she said to Magnus. 'I want to see if I can buy something special to wear to the feast tonight.'

'Alva, you are a Viking in an Anglo-Saxon city. I know you want to explore, but it is too dangerous.'

'Please, Uncle,' said Alva pleadingly. 'You can wait for me at the gate if you're worried.'

Looking concerned, Magnus reluctantly put some coins in her hand, mumbling, 'Stay safe and don't linger too long.'

As she wandered through the long, straight

streets, peering into shopfronts and taking in the sights and sounds, Alva thought that she had barely had a moment by herself since leaving Kilsgard. She liked it. She felt strong and independent. Maybe she could go after her father alone if it came to it?

One stall was selling fine silver brooches. Alva was surprised to see how much they looked like the ones worn back in Norway. Viking style was obviously fashionable. One struck her in particular. It showed a bearded face staring out from a writhing mass of serpents that interlaced around one another. Its quizzical expression reminded her of her father. 'How much?' she asked the lady behind the stall in her best attempt at Anglo-Saxon. The lady held up three fingers, and Alva passed over three small silver coins. Pleased with her purchase and tucking it inside her bag, she made her way back to the south gate to meet her uncle.

When they finally crossed into the warmth of Edwin's home she found Sigurd, Alfred, and Fenrir huddled around the fire. They all looked grumpy, apart from Fen, who bounded over, leapt up, and licked her face. She joined the sulky faces, just as Edwin bustled in with a jug of mead.

'Something to take away your frowns,' he said, pouring out cupfuls.

It was Alfred who spoke first. He seemed petulant. 'So I imagine it was amazing meeting the Queen! I've wanted to meet her for so many years, and you two can just wander in and get an audience. I would give an arm just to see her from a distance.'

'I'd like to see her so I can tell her how much suffering she has brought me,' Sigurd said darkly. 'I've waited over a year for news of my father. Now I hear Bjorn was on some "special mission", while my father was simply disposable. I wish that Thor would smash his hammer down on her Christian head.'

'Don't say that,' said Alva angrily. 'I know you're upset about your father but the Queen is not to blame. She didn't force our fathers to go on that journey. She paid them beyond measure. I am going to fetch the money she owes us tonight and will be sure to split it with you. That's only fair.'

Magnus gave a snort. 'Giving away Bjorn's money before you've even got your hands on it, Alva? I don't think that shows great wisdom, do you?'

Alva glowered at him hotter than the logs on the fire but took a deep breath and sucked her anger inwards. She knew what she was going to do now. She didn't need Magnus with her, watching her every move. He could take the Queen's money back to Kilsgard for all she cared. Once her meeting with the Queen was over, she and Fenrir would leave in the dark of night alone to search for her father. If none of these men had the courage, at least she did.

They passed an awkward few hours together. Edwin tried to lighten the atmosphere by getting Alva and Alfred to help him bake. He was an excellent cook and was crafting exquisite small biscuits, flavoured with ginger and honey, for Alva to take with her to the feast.

'You can't go to the Queen empty-handed, and my cakes are the best in town. Everyone says so. You'll see—she'll love them!' Edwin bustled over with a basket.

'Put the biscuits in here carefully,' he said. 'I will make sure they are presented in a way that befits the Lady of the Mercians.'

Magnus had stayed moody and silent throughout, at times rummaging through his bag and poring over small scraps of vellum. Sigurd stuck to the shadows, sending fiery glances in their direction while Edwin brushed leftover flour on Alva and Alfred's cheeks, making them laugh. As the sun began to set, Magnus said to Alva, 'You need to get dressed for the feast. Your finest clothes, please.' Then he stalked from the room to ready himself. Alfred, Edwin, and Sigurd were also going into town, although only the most important folk were invited to join the Queen herself in her hall while the others would stay in the square outside.

Aethelflaed had announced that day that she and all healthy men and women of Mercia who could be spared were to leave in the morning to join battle with Ragnall and his army. The whole town was bustling in preparation, loading wagons, repairing weapons, and packing for a long and arduous journey. The feast was a final send-off for those who were going to war and was meant as the Queen's gift to her people. Tables were to be set up in the market square, and everyone was to have as much food and drink as their hearts desired. Alva was excited.

Pinning on her new brooch, she thought about what she had planned for this evening. She would take some of the money promised to her by the Queen, but would leave the rest for Magnus.

Then, when everyone was sleeping, she and Fenrir would leave with Epona for the southern coast. She had her sunstone, she had her wolf, she had her wits. She would be fine. Placing her packed bag out of sight, she came back to the hearth where the others were putting the finishing touches to their outfits. Alfred looked very smart and, in the evening light, Alva thought, quite handsome. Fen was to stay at Edwin's and reluctantly agreed to being tied up near the fireplace. 'It's better than being outside,' Alva said as he whimpered at her.

Ready to leave, they made for the door. Edwin handed her the basket of biscuits, and they headed for the south gate. The guards passed them through without argument as Edwin went in front. 'Guests of mine,' he said. One of the watchmen gave him a hearty smile. The town was alive with fire and sound. Flaming torches illuminated every street and corner, while the square around the hall looked like a giant party. For those not invited to dine inside, stalls selling food and drink had popped up everywhere, with benches set out next to big fires for the people to eat in comfort. The sound of minstrels, playing lutes and pipes to the raucous crowd, made Alva's heart race.

Edwin held back with Alfred and Sigurd. Although they still looked slightly sullen, the sight of the busy market square had cheered them slightly. Alfred said to Alva, 'I hope you enjoy the feast. It looks like we will be having more fun out here though.' She took the stinging comment to heart and turned from him without saying goodbye.

She and Magnus made for the huge doors at the west end of the hall. They gave their names to the guards at the entrance, were checked off a list, then were invited inside. The hall was alive with music, although it was more stately and sedate than that in the main square. Voices blended together in a cacophony of hushed excitement. Horns of fine imported wine were being moved between the guests, and the smell of herbs and spices filled the air. There was a sense of nervous anticipation ringing through the crowd.

Magnus stayed by her side. 'Listen,' he said. 'I know you are angry with me. Believe me, there is nothing I would rather do than travel abroad in search of Bjorn . . . and treasure. But I have responsibilities. You have responsibilities. When this evening is over we make plans to join the others at Lindisfarne, and then we sail home.'

Alva gritted her teeth. She was screaming at him inside her head but stayed calm on the outside. 'Well, I've got to meet with the Queen first,' she said.

'I am anxious about that,' Magnus replied. 'Don't be entranced by her tales of your father or of the adventure she has sent him on. We are going back to Kilsgard, and that is final.'

Their conversation was cut short by a blast on a horn. Everyone went silent and turned towards the throne. Aethelflaed entered, her stunning blue gown trailing on the floor behind her, and a bejewelled crown perched high on her head. But there was a gasp as the crowd saw who followed behind her. Magnus bent down and whispered, 'That's her brother, Edward. The King of the English!'

He was all that Alva imagined a prince to be. He was tall, strong, with fire in his eyes and a bear-like stature. He carried a huge sword at his side, and the golden crown on his head was twice the size of his sister's. His face was framed with a solid brown beard, and his beautifully woven jacket was pinned with enormous brooches. Alva saw large gold finger rings on his hands, and even his shoes were threaded with golden lace. He was magnificent.

Aethelflaed went on to the platform first and addressed the room. 'My dear Mercians. My beloved people. We are here together to celebrate a most important moment in the history of the English. Tomorrow, myself and my brother, the King, will lead a huge army to the North. With the full support of the citizens of Jorvik, we will remove the tyrant ruler Ragnall and bring the city back into the open arms of the Kingdoms of England. This is an historic moment.'

Everyone cheered simultaneously, raising their glasses and pounding their feet on the floor. Then the King moved to join his sister. When he spoke, his voice was gravelly and deep. He sounded like the finest men in the hall of Kilsgard, full of fight and ferocity. 'My sister's people. You have been good and loyal to me, helping me in battle, and winning back for me the cities that had been stolen by Danes from my family. You have been rewarded, and you will be rewarded all the more. Tomorrow, we march together, men and women of Kent, Wessex, Mercia, and the North. We all want to see a good, just ruler who can carry on the work of my father. I thank you now, and when we are victorious I will thank you again tenfold!'

There were raucous cheers around the hall, and several men hammered their fists on the long benches that had been set up for the feast. Then Aethelflaed touched her brother on the arm, indicating that she had something else to add. He stepped back, and she spoke again. 'We are generous, my brother and I. Our great father taught us to reward those that deserve it. And so I want to reward two people tonight in front of you, who have done us all a magnificent service.' She lifted her hand and held aloft the roll of parchment. 'This letter here is our invitation to take back Jorvik. It was brought to us through great danger by Magnus and Alva of Kilsgard.'

As the Queen gestured towards Alva and Magnus, every head swivelled around to stare at them both. Alva felt a strong desire for the floor to open up and swallow her. The Queen continued. 'They are relatives of another fine warrior who came to us from the North and is working tirelessly for us abroad. I made that warrior a promise of great wealth. As he is not here right now to receive it, I am giving half to his brother and daughter. And for showing me such loyalty by travelling across the Kingdoms to help me, I will also reward them one hundred of my own gold coins.'

Two men came before the Queen carrying an oak box between them. Aethelflaed lifted the lid and showed the crowd the contents. There were more gold and silver coins in there than Alva had seen in her life. It was a mountain of riches. 'Alva and Magnus, please come before me.'

Feeling heat rising in her cheeks and snakes of sickness winding up her throat, Alva walked forward slowly. 'Half of these riches are yours to take away with you, and you will have one hundred gold coins from me. I will keep the other half of Bjorn's treasure safe for his return,' the Queen said to Alva and Magnus. Then she spoke loudly to the crowd. 'These are the sorts of riches you can expect if you help me and my brother defeat our enemies, strengthen our kingdom, and bring peace to our lands. You will be rewarded too! These are people from the Norse lands and we mean them no harm. It is just the tyrannical Ragnall we wish to unseat. Then Norse and Anglo-Saxon can live alongside each other.'

The cheers this time were louder than ever, each person in the hall seduced by the offers of wealth. Through the noise, Aethelflaed gestured at Magnus and Alva to follow the servants with the box from the room. A small, officious man with a tiny moustache was standing by a table in the antechamber, holding a piece of vellum on a wooden board. 'You are the relatives of Bjorn, yes?' he asked.

'We are,' Magnus replied.

'I have been instructed to give you half of this wealth in payment for services that Bjorn is rendering for the Queen.' He began to weigh the coins, placing them into piles on the table. One half of the coins he placed back into the box, locking it. He then drew out three small velvet bags and split the rest of the piles between them, before handing them to Magnus. 'And here are the additional gold coins from Queen Aethelflaed,' he added, pushing another velvet bag towards them.

'Sign your name here, please,' he said, indicating a space beneath a scrawl of writing on the vellum. Magnus took the quill and, with a practised flourish, wrote his name. 'You too,' the man said to Alva. She had tried her hand a few times at writing, but still found it difficult. Settling on runes, she scribbled the two shapes her father had used to write her name:

ᚠ ▽

Alva felt a shudder of delight as the little man

left her and her uncle cradling the three bags of coins. Magnus's eyes were alive as he spoke. 'Look, Alva! I bet you couldn't have imagined such riches when you left Kilsgard. Oh, your mother's face when she sees these . . .'

'We've got his money,' Alva said, 'but not him. This wasn't what I came abroad for.'

'This is all very overwhelming,' Magnus replied, still obviously delighted, ignoring Alva's comment. 'We need to put the treasure somewhere safe before we continue with the feast. You wait at the feast. I will ask Edwin to take me to his home and let me keep these bags in his safe-box. We don't want to lose them!' He gave a chuckle and left the hall in search of their friend.

Alva was a flurry of emotions. Sheer joy coursed through her veins at the sight of such wealth. And it was made all the sweeter in the knowledge that this was fair money, earned by her father for his efforts, and given to them in good faith by the Queen. It felt like angels had brought her to this point, and the Queen was chief amongst them. She could go back to Kilsgard rich and famous.

But she wouldn't have completed her mission. She had meant to return with her father or not at all. Alva felt she hadn't yet fulfilled her destiny.

A Slayer of Life's Duration

Alva rejoined the feast, sitting on a bench near to the Queen. As the feast went on, many people in the hall began to drink more and more of the fine wine, and their voices were raised in loud oaths. Servants moved the tables from the centre of the hall and pushed benches to the edges, then the minstrels began spinning fascinating stories of ancient English heroes, of long-lost kings, epic battles, and brave saints.

Some of the guests were making their way out of the hall, full of wine and food, desperate for a warm, soft bed before a long journey tomorrow. Alva saw the Queen was also standing to take her leave. Her brother, the King, rose too and accompanied her. Aethelflaed looked directly at Alva and raised her hand, gesturing her over. Alva gave her hands a dip in the finger bowl to clear off the last grease of the magnificent meal, straightened her wild hair as best she could, and grabbed the basket of biscuits.

As she hurried over to the Queen, she felt every nerve in her body zinging with excitement. 'Alva,' Aethelflaed said gently in Alva's Norse tongue. 'I promised you some more information about your father. Will you come with me to my chamber for a while?'

Taken aback, Alva spluttered, 'Yeah . . . I mean, yes, my lady!'

Armed guards stood in front of the door at the back of the hall, but as Alva walked behind the King and next to the Lady of the Mercians, they unlocked the doors and let them through. 'We have to keep our private chambers secure,' Aethelflaed said quietly. 'There are many people who wish me harm, particularly as we are about to go to war.'

As they wound their way along a tile-floored corridor, King Edward gestured to his sister's guest. 'Who's this?' he asked curiously.

'This is the daughter of that great Norseman,

Bjorn, who we sent on Father's mission. I owe her some answers.'

They entered her chamber past two more armed guards. The room was sumptuous and warm, with books and parchments scattered on every surface. Aethelflaed sat down on a deep red cushion, in a high-backed chair that was pressed up against a table. On another table in the centre of the room Alva saw small coloured figures lined up on top of a huge map. They were planning for battle.

Alva walked in nervously and immediately handed the basket of biscuits towards Aethelflaed. 'Edwin, Alfred, and I baked some honey and ginger biscuits for you. Here.'

'How wonderful!' the Queen said cheerfully. 'I have heard many good things about Edwin and his cooking. I must try one.' She took a biscuit from the top of the pile, putting it gracefully in her mouth. She coughed a little but politely finished the biscuit, before saying, 'Mmmm. Lovely! Won't you have one?' Alva took one but felt too nervous and excited to eat. She held it firmly in her clenched, hot hand.

'How much does the girl know of Bjorn's task?' Edward asked in Norse, so Alva understood every word.

'Nothing yet,' Aethelflaed said. 'But she has travelled from Norway here in search of him, so we should tell her where he has gone, shouldn't we?'

Edward stood by his sister, looking at Alva with great curiosity. He still had his long sword in its glittering scabbard at his side, as if it was waiting for battle. 'Your name is Alva?' he said thoughtfully. 'That means "of the elf-folk" in your tongue, I think?' Alva nodded keenly, impressed that this English king knew so much of her Viking language. 'Have you the wisdom of the elves, Alva? Or are you prone to mischief as they are?'

Alva sent a concerned glance over at Aethelflaed, unsure what to say. 'I . . .' she began. 'In my hometown I was training to be an investigator like my uncle.'

Edward gave a broad smile, pleased with this response. 'So you like a mystery then, do you?' he laughed. 'There's no bigger mystery than this. Alva, the reason your father is on this mission is that a great many things depend upon it. But it is growing late, and I have a battle to think of. I will leave my sister to tell you more.' Edward bowed courteously to Alva. 'It was a pleasure to meet a young Viking, and I can see you are a warrior woman like my sister,' he said, winking. 'You have the spirit of a shield maiden in you for sure.' With that he left the room and closed the door.

Aethelflaed patted the seat next to her and invited Alva to sit. Still clutching the sweaty biscuit in her hand, she joined the Queen. 'I'm glad I have the opportunity to speak to you alone,' Aethelflaed said in a gentle, low voice. 'You must be so concerned about your father and the mission he has left on. I want you to know that your father was concerned too. When I told him of his journey and how long he may need to search, his only worry was for you and your family. He sat here in this room and shed a tear at the thought he might not see you for some years. He cried at the thought of your mother, worrying night after night, and your uncle, who would have to take the burden of caring for you all.' She gave a sharp cough, and her cheeks flushed red. 'She must be upset,' Alva thought.

The Queen continued speaking. 'Bjorn made me swear that, if he had not returned within two years, I was to send half his money to Kilsgard.

In a twist of fate, you came to me of your own accord. I have given you his money, but more importantly I wanted to give you his love.' With this she wrapped her arms around Alva's shoulders and hugged her tight. Alva felt hot streams of tears racing down her cheeks and a gasping sensation in her chest.

'Bjorn wrote to me as he journeyed south. He would send word whenever he was near a monastery, as the monks had messengers. They were always encoded, and we had developed a way of communicating so that no one would be able to interpret the letters other than us.' Aethelflaed gave a distant smile and Alva wondered if her feelings for Bjorn were not purely of admiration. She wondered if the Queen loved her father.

'He made it through Francia, towards Tours. But while staying at a tavern, his room was ransacked. Two of his men were killed and the third vanished. Your father has continued alone and said he could no longer send letters, as someone was clearly following him.' Alva felt a sadness eating her up inside. Her father was alone, abroad, with no friends and companions. She wanted to find him even more.

'But what is this mission and when will he complete it? When can he come home?' she asked the Queen.

'It's complicated,' Aethelflaed answered. 'I will need to show you something to help explain it.' She glided over to a chest in the corner of the room. Opening it, she began rummaging through pages of vellum. As she did so she spoke over her shoulder. 'I have many ancient manuscripts that my father, King Alfred, saved from pagan fires. I share his love of learning and brought as many books here as I could when I rebuilt the palace. There are wondrous secrets hidden in here.'

The Queen was perspiring slightly as she returned to her chair with a large piece of parchment in her hands.

She rolled it out on the table. It showed a human figure wearing a simple gown. The image was well drawn, with many details picked out carefully in different coloured inks. Alva could see four coloured shapes arranged across points on the figure. A green circle hovered above one hand, a red one over his head, a blue one on his chest, and a final clear circle around his face.

As Alva looked more closely, she saw other

worrying details. The figure had blood running down from both hands and feet, and from a gash in his side. There was no cross depicted, but Alva knew who this was. It showed the one the Christians called Christ.

'There is no other known copy of this image anywhere in Christendom,' Aethelflaed said, wiping sweat from her brow. Her voice quiet and hoarse now, it was though she had been hit with a sudden exhaustion.

'But why is it so important?' Alva asked.

'Look at the coloured marks. Each represents a different precious gemstone: ruby, emerald, sapphire, and diamond. They are known as the Power Stones. They were meant to sit together in the Imperial Crown. Ancient texts record that this crown was fashioned by Saint Peter, the first Pope, himself. Whoever owned it was entitled to rule all of Christendom.

'The picture is a map telling us where the jewels and the crown are hidden. Each is connected with a particular relic associated with a different part of Christ's body: there is the famous cloth he used to wipe his face on the way to his crucifixion. The cloak that he wore on the cross, which was the only thing of value he owned. Then there are the nails that pinned his hands, and thorns from the crown that was forced on his head. Each of these relics are held in churches and monasteries across the known world.

The person who sent my father this map—Alcuin of Jorvik—was clever. He had many powerful connections, and he deliberately sent the gems far around the world so they would be kept apart until someone worthy of wielding such complete power found them. I think Alcuin sent the gems to four churches, each containing one of the relics. By searching for the relics, Bjorn can find the stones.

'Together the jewels represent the elements: water, fire, earth, and air. Together they represent pure power, for whoever owns them and the crown will have Christ on their side. My brother and I want to continue our father's good work, but we need more authority to make our kingdom great. The crown would make us most blessed and powerful rulers.'

Alva was shocked by all this information, and also felt a stab of doubt. She knew that power brought difficult choices, and the more power this warrior woman and her princely brother wielded, the harder it would be for them to stay grounded. But just as she was on a mission to find her father, so Aethelflaed was on a mission to achieve what her father wanted. Their desires were similar.

Aethelflaed began talking again. 'My father's reign was chaotic and troubled, and, despite trying, he could find no warrior worthy of the mission to retrieve the jewels and the crown. But I found your father.

'He went from here over a year ago, and although I think he is alive, I've had no news for many months now. I know, however, that he was headed first for Tours in Francia. That was Alcuin's final resting place, and Bjorn was certain he had hidden one of the gems there. From that place he will be piecing the mystery together as he travels, but it will take some detective work. At least now you know why he went, and what he is searching for.'

Alva's ears pricked up at the words 'detective work'! This was why she was here, with Magnus, in Tamworth. They were meant to complete this detective work. They were meant to follow Bjorn on this mission, and help him with it. Suddenly it all seemed clear to her. This was her destiny.

'That's the business talk done with. All of a sudden I'm feeling a little tired,' the Queen said gently. 'How about we share some of those biscuits before I start a long night of war preparations with my brother?' Alva lifted the basket to the table, and the Queen reached in for another. Alva lifted her slightly soggy biscuit to her mouth, mirroring Aethelflaed. But as she went to take a bite, Alva saw the Queen's expression change. She took a sudden rasping breath, threw her hands to her neck, and fell to the floor. She bent over, and Alva heard choking sounds.

Leaping to her feet, Alva ran to the side of the Lady of the Mercians and placed a hand on her shoulder. 'What's wrong? How can I help?' The Queen began pulling frantically at her belt and drew out her paring knife. Alva jumped back, afraid the Queen was going to stab her in a fit of madness. But instead, she began carving at the floor next to her. 'What's happening?' Alva asked, terrified. 'Speak to me!' But the Queen kept gasping for breath and scratching feverishly. Her body was convulsing in spasms. Then the choking stopped, and Aethelflaed fell face down. Alva stood frozen in complete shock.

It had happened so fast that she couldn't even cry out for help.

Placing a hand on Aethelflaed's back, Alva felt the Queen's body go rigid beneath her fingers. She turned her over. But the life had left Aethelflaed like a trapped bird escaping through a window. There was nothing left in her eyes. She was dead. Alva was cold with fear. What had happened? She looked around the room, searching for some clues as to how and why the Queen had died. A chilling thought passed through her: she would be the main suspect!

She had to find out more, quickly, before anyone else arrived. She took a quick look around the room and saw the basket of biscuits. Crawling closer to Aethelflaed, she looked at the Queen intently. She picked up a few crumbs that were lying near her hand and held them up to her nose. There was a faintly acrid smell and some yellow staining on her fingers. Could the Queen have been poisoned? And if so, was it the biscuits? Her biscuits? The cups were clean, so she hadn't drunk anything in here that could have been laced with poison. She'd been fine when they entered the room, but become increasingly flushed and feverish while they talked together. The only thing she had eaten was the biscuits Alva herself had brought. It was all her fault!

Quickly, she picked up the parchment from the table, rolled it up, and slipped it in her bag. She knew she was now adding theft to her list of crimes, but this was the only thing she had that could tell her where to search for her father.

Next, she began examining the area around the Queen. What had Aethelflaed been carving into the floor? At first it looked simply like a collection of random shapes, but Alva thought this could be a valuable clue. Grabbing a quill and parchment from a table, she copied down the shapes hurriedly. She took the crumbs from the Queen's hand and put those in her bag too.

But Alva's time investigating was up. There was a knock at the door and a horrified gasp from the King as he stepped into the room to find his sister lying on the floor and Alva rummaging around next to her. He fell to his knees, shouting, 'Aethelflaed? Aethelflaed, wake up!' Slowly it dawned on him that his sister was dead. He went silent before letting out a mighty cry of pain. Guards rushed into the room the second his howl expired. They took one look at the Queen then made for Alva. As they pulled her to her feet she began trying to explain, 'I . . . it was the biscuits . . . it wasn't me.' But her words were drowned by the guards. 'Is this down to you, filthy Viking?' one spat. 'She's poisoned the Queen!' another shouted.

'I didn't kill her,' Alva tried again, but now her voice was lost beneath the howls and shrieks of more people who had begun piling into the small room. A handmaid fell down in a dead faint, while bodies began swimming in and out of the room. 'Stop, you'll ruin the evidence,' Alva protested, but no one heard her. The King got to his feet, now burning with the rage of a volcano. 'Did you do this?' he said, pointing to Alva.

'I . . . I . . .' Alva spluttered, but she couldn't get her words out. For once, her courage had abandoned her.

Drink of the Vǫlsungar

'Lock her up,' the King commanded, and before she knew what was happening, strong arms had seized Alva, pulling her through the corridor and out into a courtyard. Cold air hit her hard in the face, and she felt suddenly dizzy. She lost her footing, but the guards simply continued dragging her along the ground. They went out a side gate of the courtyard and into another enclosure. It was ringed with a high wooden fence, and at one end was a small hut with a huge bolt on the door. The guards said nothing but unlocked the door and threw her inside. One spat at her as he was leaving, and then she was plunged into darkness.

'What's happening?' Alva asked through

tears. 'I didn't do anything.' She sat shivering and sobbing as silence surrounded the outside of her cell. Then after a few moments she heard new sounds. The guards were back, this time dragging someone who was protesting and shouting in strong, loud Anglo-Saxon. It was Magnus. They had Magnus!

The door flew open, and the guards let go of Magnus. He stood, brushed down his beard, straightened his cloak, and said, 'You are so wrong. You will realize soon, you are so wrong.' Then he willingly stepped inside the cell. Alva shot to her uncle, throwing her arms around him as more tears surged from her eyes. 'I'm so sorry you're in here,' she heaved. 'It's the Queen. She's dead. They think it was me!'

'Oh, Alva,' Magnus replied through the darkness. 'It's always one setback after another for us.' He chuckled quietly and sorrowfully.

'But you know I wasn't involved, don't you?' Alva asked tearfully.

'Of course I do, Alva. But you need to tell me everything you know so that we can plead with the King and get out of here. They will hang us at dawn if not.'

Hang us? Well of course they would be

hanged. She had killed a rightful ruler. She had set back the war with Ragnall. She was a Viking, trusted by the Queen, who seemed to have taken advantage of her kindness to kill her. This was just too awful.

'Alva,' Magnus said breathlessly, 'I know you are upset, but you must try and remember every detail. It could help to save us. Show me you are an investigator.'

Taking a deep breath, she thought back to the crime scene, her weeping settling as she turned her mind to work.

'I went back to Aethelflaed's chamber after the feast with her and the King while you were hiding our money at Edwin's. Her rooms are behind the great hall, with two sets of locked doors, both manned by two guards each. King Edward came with us into the chamber.'

'Ah yes, the King,' Magnus said thoughtfully. 'It could be him, you know. He may have wanted his sister gone so he could wield power over Wessex AND Mercia. Perhaps he wanted the sole glory of taking Jorvik? As King, he's always been in his sister's shadow.'

'No, I don't think that's the case. I think it was the biscuit that killed her, and Edward didn't go near them.'

'Why do you think it was the biscuits?' Magnus asked, shocked by this revelation.

'She ate one as soon as we went into the room, then as we talked she began to cough and seemed to be getting hot and flustered. I picked up some crumbs from the floor, and I think they smell strange.' Alva reached into her bag and drew out the fragments, passing them to her uncle. Magnus sniffed them, and Alva could just make out a knowing look passing over his features in the darkness.

'This is good detective work, Alva,' he said. 'What else can you tell me?'

'The Queen was getting worse and worse the longer we talked, but I didn't realize anything was wrong until she grabbed at her throat and fell to the floor choking. Then she took out her knife and started scratching shapes into the floor. It was so weird!'

'Please tell me you remember the symbols,' Magnus said.

'I did even better,' replied Alva confidently. 'I scribbled them down.' She reached into her bag once again and brought out the scrap of vellum. Magnus's eyes widened in appreciation as he took it from her hands and moved towards the crack of light creeping in under the door.

The first shape was a large X. The symbol next to it showed a set of three triangles overlapping each other.

'That's the *valknut*,' Alva said, pointing to the second image. 'It's Odin's knot. Aethelflaed must have been trying to say that her death was down to Vikings. This doesn't look good for us!'

'But what about the first symbol?' Magnus asked.

'It looks like "Gifu", the rune for a gift,' Alva said, straining to see it in the darkness. 'It could be that Aethelflaed is saying it's the Viking gift that has killed her.'

'But this means something else in magical circles, Alva,' Magnus continued. 'It can also mean "protection against poison". Was she scared she was being poisoned? Then there are the crumbs from the biscuit. Take a look.' He held up the crumbs again. 'It's difficult to make out in here, but when you were in the Queen's chamber, did you see any unusual colour on the crumbs?'

Alva replied cautiously, 'I'm not entirely sure . . . But I think—well to me at least—that the

crumbs looked slightly yellow.'

'That's it, Alva!' Magnus exclaimed excitedly. 'I am certain they have been sprinkled with orpiment.'

Alva looked confused, so Magnus continued. 'Orpiment has many uses, particularly in scribal work, where it makes a lovely golden colour on parchment. But it is also misused as a poison. It can be ground down and purified, so that if it is eaten it will cause death very quickly. The biscuits were poisoned, Alva. But by whom?'

'I don't think it was her brother, and I certainly didn't do it,' Alva said. 'Who else wanted her dead?' Then she felt realization like a clanging bell in her brain. 'Ragnall!' she shouted. 'Ragnall wanted her dead! He feared going to war against her and would rather she never make it to Jorvik.'

'Right,' said Magnus. 'But as you said, there was no one else in the room. Who put the purified orpiment on to the biscuits?'

Alva thought backwards through her evening. She had a hand on the basket of biscuits at all times, through the feast and up to the point when she met with the Queen. The only time she had been away from them was inside Edwin's house. 'Oh no,' she said, her heart sinking. 'They must have been poisoned just after we baked them.'

Magnus nodded in the darkness. Alva continued speaking. 'So that means one of our friends must have done this. Could it have been Edwin? He was only looking after us because Father Michael told him to. Perhaps he hated the Queen? It couldn't be Alfred. I just can't imagine that. Or what about . . .' Another clanging sense of realization. She fell silent for a moment, then quietly whispered, 'It was Sigurd.'

Magnus drew towards her in the dark and put his hand on her knee, waiting for her to speak more. 'It has to be Sigurd,' she said sadly. 'He had plenty of opportunity to poison them, and he knew I was taking them to the Queen. And he had the motive. He blamed Aethelflaed for his father's death.'

Alva fell silent, then Magnus said, 'I suspected he might have been working for Ragnall when he arrived in Tamworth. I knew Ragnall would send spies after us, but I did not think he would be able to recruit one of our own men. Sigurd has been missing a strong father figure this past year. It's very possible he saw in Ragnall something to be admired. And I'm sure he was offered lots of money for his efforts. Remember, he too has a family to provide for back in Kilsgard.'

'Sigurd had a double motive,' Alva said thoughtfully. 'On the one hand, he could do Ragnall's wishes, poison the Queen, and get rich. On the other, he could find the truth about his father's whereabouts. It's not dissimilar to you and I. After all, we knew we'd be paid for taking the letter, and we wanted to know more about my father.'

Alva felt such sadness at this realization. She had known Sigurd her whole life. Along with Ingeld, his father Ulf had been Bjorn's best friend in Kilsgard. There was rarely a family get-together when Sigurd didn't dance around, entertaining the children, or play like a fool on the floor of their home, messing about with Fenrir. But it could only be him that had poisoned the Queen.

'What do we do?' Alva asked. 'Sigurd is back at Edwin's hut by now. Oh, by the gods! What if he takes our money and escapes? What about Edwin, and Alfred, and Fen . . .?'

'We must get out of here,' Magnus said hurriedly. 'We have to get the guards' attention and tell them what we know. You've got to help me, Alva. We have to make as much noise as possible.' He began shaking the hut, banging on the walls, and howling. Alva joined in, and together they made a noise that would have shaken the giants from their slumber.

Angry voices approached the hut and, after the rattling of a key in the lock, the moonlight, seemingly bright as the sun, poured into the hut. Magnus spoke quickly and calmly in Anglo-Saxon. 'You must let us show you the evidence we have. We know who killed the Queen, and he has escaped. If you don't let us out now, he could kill more people and you will never get justice.'

The guards exchanged a confused look for a moment. Magnus spoke again, 'You perhaps saw the Queen give me and my niece here many bags worth of coins in payment for the service we had done her. If you take us before King Edward for just a few moments, then I will reward you handsomely with gold.'

'I did see him get all those riches,' the taller of the two guards said, thoughtfully. 'The King is distraught and surely will want to know any information they have has about what happened to his sister. Also, if we get this wrong and another criminal is riding away from Tamworth, it will be us on the gallows tomorrow morning. You promise to pay us?' he said back at Magnus. Her uncle gave a solemn nod of his head. They pulled Alva and Magnus from the prison cell and said, 'Come with us. This needs to be resolved.' They all traipsed back towards the palace, where the King was pacing up and down in the courtyard, his face distorted with weeping.

Edward looked devastated and threw his weary limbs down on to a bench. He exploded at Alva, 'I don't want to see you now, murderer.'

Magnus came forward quickly. 'My condolences, my lord,' he said, bowing low. 'Your sister was an unparalleled jewel and a wise woman in a wicked world. But I implore you, listen to what we have to say. Alva was not responsible for your sister's death, and the real murderer could be escaping from Tamworth as we speak.' The King grunted, paused, and then nodded slowly, urging Magnus to continue. 'I'll let Alva explain this to you, as she is the one who holds all the clues to understanding what happened.'

Giving her an encouraging look, Magnus stepped away. All eyes on her, Alva cleared her throat and rooted herself to the spot. 'My lord,' she began, 'I feel a huge burden of guilt for what has happened to your sister tonight. If I had not been in her chamber, then she would still be alive. I must take some responsibility, but it was not me who killed her.

'When we left Jorvik we were sure that Ragnall would send someone after us. He wanted our fellow men of Kilsgard to act as spies for him, which is why we all needed to escape quickly. After a long and difficult journey to Tamworth we found refuge at the home of Edwin, just outside the south gate. It was while we were staying there that one of our fellow Norsemen came into the hut. His name is Sigurd, and he was my dear friend. His father Ulf travelled with mine on the mission your sister and I spoke of tonight. I thought he had come south for the same reason as me: to find out what happened to his father.'

Alva continued talking, her confidence rising with each moment that passed. 'Sigurd was distraught to discover that his father had been killed while on the Queen's mission. I think this is what persuaded him to commit the murder that Ragnall had paid him for. He did this by lacing my gift to the Queen, the biscuits, with a deadly poison. If this is true, we think he will have travelled to Edwin's hut, to claim Bjorn's treasure for himself and ride north to Ragnall.'

The King sat silenced by Alva's speech. Magnus gave her shoulder a firm squeeze, looking down proudly at her. Edward thought for a moment, then called a guard over. 'Do you know this Edwin and where he lives?'

'We can take you there,' Magnus interjected.

Thinking again for a moment, the King suddenly leaped to his feet. 'We travel with many guards immediately,' he said in a loud voice. More men in arms appeared, and in what seemed like seconds, Alva, Magnus, and the King of England were leaving the city, headed for Edwin's hut.

The Roof-Ridge of the Temple of the Ground

As they walked towards the hut, Alva could hear a sound that pained her heart. Fenrir was howling. He was tied up around the back, padding frantically and trying to break the rope with his teeth. 'Fen,' she shouted, flying to his side. Fenrir gave her face a happy lick but continued pulling on the rope. Alva untied him, and he immediately ran past the guards and towards the front door, where he began scratching feverishly.

'My wolf can sniff out crime,' Alva said proudly. 'If he wants to get inside, then we all should follow.' The door was unlocked, and as Alva pushed it open Fenrir flew into the darkness. From inside, Alva could hear a muffled voice. 'Good boy, Fen.' It was Alfred. He was alive.

The guards brought lit torches inside, and such a scene of chaos met their eyes that Alva didn't know where to look first. In the centre of the floor lay Edwin, face down, with a pool of blood seeping from his head. Alfred was tied to a chair by the fire, and the whole room had been turned upside down. Rushes had been ripped up from the floor, pieces of wood had been heaved from the walls, and baskets, pots, and pans lay strewn across the floor.

'What in God's name has happened here?' King Edward asked. He had pushed through past the guards and now stood staring around in shock. Alfred spoke quietly, 'It was Sigurd. He came back to the hut a little while after Edwin and I had returned from the celebrations. He was in a fury and began tearing the house apart. Edwin asked him what he was looking for, and he said he wanted his share of Magnus and Alva's blood money. Edwin refused to tell him where it was hidden so Sigurd began beating him. I tried to stop him, but he tied me up. Fenrir got really angry when he saw Sigurd hurting me and bit him on the arm. Sigurd dragged Fen from the hut and tied him up outside, but then he must have heard you approaching because he didn't come back in. Instead I heard him leap on one of the horses and ride away. He left just moments ago!'

As Alfred spoke, Magnus released his bonds, now he knelt down by Edwin, tending to his wounds. He was alive, but very groggy. One of the guards found a cup of ale and brought it over. Edwin took a few long glugs and seemed to recover slightly.

'Edwin,' Magnus said quietly, 'is what Alfred says true?'

Wiping blood from his face, Edwin spoke slowly. 'Sigurd was wild with fear. He said he had done something that would see him hanged and he had to leave Tamworth immediately. I asked what could be so bad that he would be punished with death, and he told me he had poisoned the biscuits I'd made for the Queen.' Edwin spluttered and choked, and Alva fell on her knees next to him, hugging him tight.

Releasing Edwin, she saw Sigurd's bag lying in the corner and went over to it. Perhaps it contained more clues. She turned the contents out on to the table. Inside was a letter. Alva unfurled it and passed it to her uncle. Magnus, looking surprised, read it then spoke up loudly.

'My niece has found a message here from Ragnall, signed by Sigurd. It promises payment of one hundred gold coins upon successful completion of his "mission to Tamworth".' Also lying on the table next to Sigurd's possessions was a small empty glass vial. Magnus lifted it to his nose and nodded. 'Orpiment. Just as I thought. A deadly poison that would have acted fast.'

Magnus addressed the King. 'Alva did not kill your sister. Here is all your proof. The man who poisoned her is currently riding away in great haste towards Jorvik. If you send your guards on horseback at once, you can catch up with him.'

The King sat down heavily on a stool, sighing at Magnus's words. 'You heard him,' he said to the two nearest guards. 'Take horses and catch me this murderer.' They ran from the room, and almost immediately Alva heard hooves pounding the track outside.

Edward looked deep into Alva's eyes. She could see a part of his soul lay crushed inside. To lose any sister must be torment. But to lose one who was his ally and, indeed, his superior in so many things must have been devastating. 'I want you to leave here with my blessing, Alva,' he said eventually. 'I should have trusted that the daughter of Bjorn would not turn against my sister. It is not you I am enraged with. It's not even that poor Viking who administered the poison. It is Ragnall. And I will use that anger when I head north tomorrow with my army. But news of my sister's death will bring chaos to the kingdoms. You must not travel north. No safety lies that way.'

His expression suddenly changed, and he looked more intently at Alva. 'You said you were an investigator? How do you feel about helping your father with his investigations? This mission is more important now than ever. I will give you all you need and send you safely on your way. I will also ensure that your money gets back to Kilsgard so your mother and brother will be taken care of. What do you think?'

Alva looked at Magnus. His face slowly broke into an anxious smile. 'Well, we cannot return to the North while war rages,' Magnus said. 'We can trust that the King of England will find a way to ensure our money gets safely back to Brianna and Ivan. And I have to admit, throughout all of this I have been desperate to find out more about the adventure Bjorn has been sent on. If it's a true mystery then we surely can't let it lie. After all,' he winked at Alva, 'we are investigators! You must tell me all you know, niece, if I am to follow you on this mission.'

But their conversation was cut short by the sound of horses whinnying outside the hut. Men's raised voices and scuffles of feet could be heard, and a moment later the door flew open. Framed in the moonlight stood a dishevelled-looking Sigurd, blood running from his nose and hair ruffled like a lion's mane around his head.

'He had hardly left the town,' one of the guards said. 'The horse was trying to buck him off, and we took him down with very little effort.' He gave Sigurd a whack around the head, then pushed him towards the King. Alva could see that his hands were bound behind his back.

Sigurd fell to his knees before the King, who rose up and drew his sword in response. 'You are the murderer,' Edward said in a terrifyingly calm voice. 'You poisoned my sister?'

'Yes, my lord,' Sigurd whimpered. He had clearly been beaten by the guards, but Alva thought that his greatest pain was raging inside. He was guilty and scared.

'Why did you do it?' Alva shrieked, running

forward and pressing her face up close to his.

'Step back, Alva,' Magnus warned, but she pulled Sigurd's chin up with both hands and held his gaze. 'She was a great woman. Why do it?'

'You know why,' Sigurd replied sorrowfully. 'Ragnall promised me one hundred gold coins. I could have returned to my family a rich man and looked after my mother and sister through many winters. But more than that I wanted to punish her. Nothing can replace my father, and it was she who sent him to his death. How would you feel if she had done that to Bjorn? Wouldn't you want revenge?'

They looked deeply into each other's eyes a moment longer, and Alva knew he had read her soul. Of course she would have wanted revenge. She was a Viking after all. Letting his face drop, she walked slowly back to Magnus.

'You have let all the people of Kilsgard down with your actions, Sigurd,' her uncle boomed. 'You followed a bad lord, and you must face the consequences of your actions.'

The King was nodding as Magnus spoke, but Alva felt a rush of sorrow pour through her blood—she couldn't watch her old friend hang. Tears were rolling down Sigurd's cheeks, and he cried out to all in the hut, 'Forgive me! I was blinded by lust for riches and the desire for revenge. Please, Magnus, Alva, forgive me!'

Alva felt such pity for him, and she could see that the King too was moved by his tears. Moving slowly to Edward, she pulled at his arm to whisper in his ear. 'My lord, I will go on this dangerous journey for you, and my father, uncle, and I will bring back your crown. But please show mercy to Sigurd. Do not disgrace his name. By all means imprison him, but please send his father's money back to his family at the same time as you return mine. His mother and sister do not need to suffer. And they need know nothing of how he has tarnished his reputation. Let him die quietly and unknown, but let his name live on in the minds of those who loved him.'

Edward recoiled at this, pushed Alva away, and began pacing up and down the hut. 'Please, my lord,' Alva continued. 'Doesn't your religion teach that forgiveness is the most precious virtue? We Vikings could learn from that, as we wrap ourselves up in feuds that can destroy entire families. Couldn't you be that just ruler who offers some forgiveness?'

Magnus looked furious, but Alva could see her words were hitting home with the King. 'My sister was unlike any other woman,' Edward was saying quietly. 'She had the strength of ten men and the brains of many more. This man took her life for cruel and selfish reasons.'

Pausing again, he looked into the flames of the fire. 'But I do accept that he was simply the puppet. It is at Ragnall's feet I lay the blame, and if I can exercise forgiveness here tonight, that means I can wreak my revenge fully on him. What do you propose, Alva? The man must be punished, after all!'

'Enslave him,' Alva said. 'He can make good for his actions, working here for the people of Tamworth. Slowly and over many years, he will pay for his crime.'

Edwin was sitting up now and listening to the conversation. 'I would gratefully enslave him, my lord,' he said. 'He has caused me much pain tonight, but I can make him work tirelessly for me. I will make him pay his dues.'

The King still looked anxious. 'My nobles will want to know how and why the Queen died,' he said. 'What can I tell them?'

Now Magnus spoke calmly and authoritatively from the shadows. 'My niece has proposed something extraordinary tonight, my lord. Our people seek revenge with an unquenchable thirst, so for you to spare Sigurd's life would be an incredible act. But I do think her suggestion has merits. It is Ragnall you seek for your sister's death. Sigurd was a pawn in a larger game. Tying him for life to Edwin will enable him to be much more useful to you alive than dead.'

Alva added, 'And it is the condition that we require if you want us to travel onwards and help with your mission. Sigurd is enslaved. His family's wealth is returned to Kilsgard. Then we find your Power Stones and your crown.'

Edward had been staring into the fire throughout these speeches while Sigurd grovelled and whimpered near his feet. Turning towards them, the King said, 'Okay, I agree. No one will know the true way my sister met her death. I will say she died suddenly in the night. But I do this on the promise that you return to me with the crown of all crowns. Are we in agreement?' Alva and the King took each other by the hand, and so the agreement was sealed.

Punisher of Discord, Nourisher of Wisdom

A week later, Magnus and Alva stood looking out over cliffs as white as a dove's feathers. 'We made it to the coast,' Alva said proudly.

Magnus looked down affectionately at her, ruffling her wild red hair with his slim hand. 'You've done so well, Alva,' he said kindly. 'I still think it was a bad idea for you to have left Kilsgard in the first place. But there is no one I'd rather be with right now.' He put his wide, strong arms around her, and they stood still, on top of the world, holding each other.

'What about me?' Alfred said, running over with Fenrir. 'Wouldn't you like to be right here with me too?' Alva gave a giggle and threw a friendly arm around Alfred's shoulders. He had insisted on travelling with them, since he couldn't return to Jorvik either while the kingdoms were at war.

Edward had been true to his word. Sigurd had been deprived of all his goods and enslaved to Edwin, with shackles around his ankles to prevent him ever trying to escape again. Alva had looked back sorrowfully as they left Edwin and Sigurd for the last time but felt that the kindness that pulsed deep in both their hearts would eventually allow them to live happily alongside each other.

In the following days, Alva had gone over every detail she knew of the mission her father had been sent on. She showed her uncle the parchment, explained that they had to travel across Christendom to different locations, and that their goal was four precious jewels and a crown. Magnus was delighted at the adventure, but baffled by its complexity. 'This is too difficult, Alva,' he had said. 'We will have to travel many miles, and we won't be safe.' But Alva felt sure they would find her father and together they could solve this ultimate mystery.

The King had provided strong, capable

horses for Magnus and Alfred, but Alva had chosen to stick with Epona. While she was small and needed some nourishment, Alva was fond of the gentle little horse and had sent Alfred's aunt enough gold coins to buy her. Edwin had given them the three bags of coins he had hastily buried at the root of an oak tree in his garden after the feast. They took one bag with them and entrusted the other two to King Edward, who swore he would send messengers that very day to Kilsgard with the parcel of riches.

Alva wanted to include something with the coins so her mother would know that she was okay. In the fresh morning air, as they were readying themselves to leave Tamworth, she had found a rose bush, bursting into colour in the mid-Spring light. She plucked one of the bright red roses, took a pebble from the ground nearby, and on it carved her two runes. Tucking these inside one of the bags, she hoped her mother would understand the love she was sending home over the waves.

Now they stood staring into more waves. But these did not lead north to the forests of Kilsgard, home-made stew, and cuddles with her little brother. These led to the unknown.

As they looked out over Dover's cliffs, Alfred slipped his hand into Alva's. 'We are off on an adventure!' he said, his grin like a crescent moon. The boat that was to transport them across the waters to Francia was pulling up on the shore below. Alfred and Magnus ran down the steep banks to meet it, but Alva stayed a moment longer on the clifftop with Fenrir.

She looked into the pale blue sky as clouds buffered across it in patterns and shapes. One melded into the form of a woman, white gown and long hair billowing behind her as she soared across the sky. Alva looked hard at it, contemplating how she might follow in the footsteps of that most wondrous Saxon queen she had had the pleasure of being with for such a short time. Fen licked the inside of her hand affectionately, and she turned her eyes from the sky to the earth, and then to the water. She needed to be strong where she was going. But she couldn't be strong without friendship, love, and support. As she grabbed Fenrir by his big fluffy mane and climbed down towards the happy calls of Alfred and Magnus, she felt loved. One adventure was ending, but she was sure another was just beginning.

KENNINGS KEY

A kenning was a type of phrase used by Vikings to describe something, like a tree or the sun, in a poetic way. You may have noticed that all of the chapter titles in this book are kennings. If not, now is the perfect time to go back and take a look. See if you can guess the kennings' meanings before looking at this key.

KENNING	MEANING
The Moon's Wheel *Mána hvéls*	Night
Horse of the Mountains of the Swans *Hestar svanfjalla*	Ship
The Fish Field *Iyteigs*	Sea
The Heart of the Earth *Hnegg folder*	Gemstone
Wide Awning of the Cloud Halls *Víðu tjaldi skyranna*	Sky
Fair Jewel of the High Storm-House *Fagrgims hás hreggranns*	Sun
Terrifying Lord of Princes *Ægr þengill jöfra*	King

KENNING	MEANING
Servants of the Son of Mary *þrælar sonar Máríu*	Christians
Diminisher of Falsehoods *þverris svika*	Virtuous Ruler
Timber-Fast Boat of the Building Plot *Timbrfastr nǫkkvi toptar*	Houses
Bold Enjoyer of the Glory *Snjallr njótr veg*	Viking Ruler
The Highest Mind-Board *Hæst hugborð*	Courage
Rowing of Wind-Oars *Róðri vindára*	Flight
Of the Seaweed of the Hill-Slope *þangs hlíðar*	Forest
Saddle-Beasts *Sǫðuldýrum*	Horses

KENNING	MEANING
Of the Stream of the Land of the Snowdrift of the Earth *Skafls jarðar hauðrs run*	River
Hall of the Sun's Stronghold *Salr sólborgar*	Earth
Beautifully Dressed Oak of Riches *Fagrbúin eik aura*	Woman
A Slayer of Life's Duration *Felli lífdvalar*	Death
People of the Moon's Path *þjóðar mána stiettar*	Angels
Drink of the Vǫlsungar *Drekku Vǫlsunga*	Poison
The Roof-Ridge of the Temple of the Ground *Mœni hofs moldar*	Zenith/ Highest Point
Punisher of Discord, Nourisher of Wisdom *Hegnir rógs, grœðir vísdóms*	Just Ruler

VIKING GLOSSARY

CONSTANTINOPLE

Istanbul in Turkey was called Constantinople between 330 and 1453, and was once the capital of the Roman Empire.

FRANCIA

A large kingdom in western Europe made up of parts of modern-day France, Belgium, and Germany.

FREYA

The goddess of love. She wears a cloak made from falcon feathers and rides into battle on a chariot pulled by cats.

FREYR

The god of peace, twin brother of Freya, and ruler of the elves.

JARL

A chief and wealthy nobleman who rules over a Viking territory.

JORVIK

The Viking name for the English city of York. It was originally founded by the Romans as 'Eboracum'.

LINDISFARNE

A small island off the coast of north-east England, home to Christian monks. It is known as the site of an infamous Viking raid in 793.

LOKI

The god of mischief and mayhem—a cunning trickster and shape-shifter.

MERCIA

One of the most powerful kingdoms of Anglo-Saxon Britain.

NORNS

The three goddesses of destiny, who weave the strands of life, deciding the fate of all living beings.

ODIN

Ruler of all the gods, sometimes known as the All-Father. He rides on an eight-legged horse called Sleipnir.

SUNSTONE

A Viking navigation tool, allowing seafarers to locate the sun in an overcast sky.

SVEFNTHORN

The *svefnthorn* or 'sleep thorn' is a magical symbol that can cast a spell of deep sleep.

THOR

The hammer-wielding god of thunder, known for his great strength.

VALHALLA

Half of the Viking warriors who die in battle are chosen to spend their afterlife in Valhalla, an enormous hall, ruled over by the god Odin.

VALKYRIES

The Valkyries or 'choosers of the slain' fly over battlefields on their horses. They choose the most heroic of the dead and take them to Valhalla.

WORLD TREE

Known as Yggdrasil, this immense ash tree connects the nine worlds of Norse mythology. Dragons, eagles, and stags are said to live in its branches.

The adventure continues . . .

Join Alva as she sails to Francia in search of her father. Will the hunt for relics lead to Bjorn, or will she find herself facing more mysteries?

David Wyatt began illustrating at the age of seventeen, working for British comic 2000AD. He has worked on books by many authors including Philip Pullman, Terry Pratchett, Diana Wynne-Jones and Philip Reeve He lives on Dartmoor where the ancient environment provides endless inspiration for historical and mythical images. Recently he won the Blue Peter Book of the Year for his work on Kieran Larwood's Podkin One-Ear.

Janina Ramirez is a cultural historian and broadcaster who specializes in decoding symbols and uncovering the bigger picture behind works of art and literature.

She is course director for the Undergraduate Certificate in History of Art at Oxford University, and has been writing and presenting history programmes for BBC television and radio since 2010. She has a weekly podcast, *Art Detectives* produced by History Hit. She has also written a number of academic books and articles on the early medieval period.

She lives in Oxfordshire with her husband, son, daughter, and two cats. When she gets a quiet moment (rarely!) she likes to listen to audiobooks, play with dolls' houses, and watch old episodes of *Inspector Morse.*

Have you read Riddle of the Runes?

Alva rushes through the trees
in the dead of night with her
sniffer wolf, Fen.
Being out alone when there's a
kidnapper on the loose is reckless,
but if she ever wants to be
an investigator like her
Uncle Magnus, she'll need to be
first to the crime scene.

But what Alva discovers
raises more questions than
it answers, drawing her into
a dangerous search for truth,
and for treasure . . .

'A ferocious heroine as strong as steel—and a
mystery worthy of her skills. You'll love it.'
Lucy Worsley

'A tale with a big, warm, wild heart.' Frank Cottrell Boyce

JANINA RAMIREZ

RIDDLE OF THE RUNES

A VIKING MYSTERY

ILLUSTRATED BY DAVID WYATT

Turn the page to read an extract

Alva shuddered as the twinned voices of her uncle and the monk died down. This tale was fascinating! A secret casket covered with codes that needed deciphering. Travellers across seas searching for hidden treasure. A lone figure attacking men on the mountain and dragging them away. It was the stuff of Alva's dreams and yet it was unfolding right now. Her body thrummed with excitement and fear.

Another voice spoke up. 'But why should we waste our time on this English monk?'

Magnus spoke with anger. 'Can't you see the importance of this? A man is missing on our mountain. He was attacked and dragged away. This means there is a kidnapper, or potentially a murderer, roaming the outskirts of Kilsgard. We have to protect the people, and to do that, we have to unpick the strands of this story.'

'Ha ha!' thought Alva, 'I'm just the person to unravel this mystery. Magnus will definitely need my help tonight!'

Magnus continued speaking behind the wall of oak, 'Jarl Erik, we must treat the monk as a guest of this hall. His people have been attacked by our people, and it took courage to come here in the death of night. You should set up safe quarters for him outside, since he will not want to sleep inside the hall with the men.'

Alva heard the familiar and warm tones of Jarl Erik. 'Magnus, you are the best at leading such investigations. You shall take two of my karls with you to the place the monk said he was attacked, and then you can test the truth of his words.' A slight grumble murmured through the hall. Alva knew the men would not be pleased that Magnus was yet again being shown special favour by the jarl.

The conversation shifted to discussing where the man should sleep, who should support his claim for hostage rights, and who should travel with Magnus. Stepping away from the doorway, Alva rapidly turned over the monk's story in her mind. She knew she should creep back to bed. Her mother was so tired, because Ivan had a touch of elf-shot and had been screaming in pain for the last few nights. She should do the right thing and be ready to help at daybreak. But then Alva saw the monk's travelling cloak lying by the entrance, and the decision crystallized in her mind. The mystery was too much temptation for her.

She was going to help her uncle unravel the

monk's story. Magnus was taking too long, discussing all the details and worrying over the visitor. She had to move fast, as clues could be lost if they delayed. Hadn't he told her that himself? Grasping the monk's cloak, she rubbed its scent under Fenrir's muzzle. 'Follow,' she said, and the silver wolf set off at once, leading her deep into the forest.

The main gates of the town were unguarded, because all the karls had rushed to the hall when the stranger arrived. There was a long pathway which ran along the river. It branched off after a few hundred paces, with one road leading out to the north, and a second winding up towards Giant's Finger.

The mountain looked silent and brooding in the moonlight. It had many moods, and Alva knew them all. She spent more time exploring its rocks and crevices than was normal for a girl of her age. In her twelve winters, she had been drawn back to the mountain time and again, in search of evidence for the tales her people told of the Great Battle, when giants and dwarves carved out the landscape.

She wanted to believe these myths, but her keen eyes found no sign of the tens of thousands of bodies that were supposed to lie at the root of the mountain. Alva always believed what her eyes saw over what her ears heard. But recently she had been drawn to the mountain for another reason—for the connection it held with her father. They had walked here together before he left, and here she could feel a little closer to him, as well as escaping the tense atmosphere of the family home.

Alva carried on running up the steep slopes of Giant's Finger, as the main route twisted away from the high incline. Her mind wasn't on where she was going, after all she had climbed these paths hundreds of times before. Instead she thought about her uncle and the tensions that had been increasing within their once close little family. When her father was in Kilsgard everyone was happy. He would take her on adventures. Magnus would occupy her with stories from his travels and insights into the many mysteries he'd solved. Her mother would gently chide both men for the way they treated Alva like their equal. But since father had left the mood was very different . Why was there so much quiet hostility in her home?

Here are some other stories we think you'll love . . .